A Suitable Husband

A Suitable Husband

Fenella-Jane Miller

ROBERT HALE · LONDON

ISBN-10: 0-7090-8029-8
ISBN-13: 978-0-7090-8029-9

Robert Hale Limited
Clerkenwell House
Clerkenwell Green
London EC1R 0HT

2 4 6 8 10 9 7 5 3 1

Typeset in 11½/14½pt Palatino
by Derek Doyle & Associates, Shaw Heath.
Printed in Great Britain by St Edmundsbury Press,
Bury St Edmunds, Suffolk.
Bound by Woolnough Bookbinding Ltd.

For my wonderful children, Annabel and Lincoln
who have filled my life with joy and love.

Chapter One

SARAH frowned. It was too late to change her mind for the hired chaise was at that very moment bowling up to the front door. Unwilling to be seen by her visitor gawping like a village urchin, she stepped back and thus failed to see the occupant of the vehicle descend. If she had done so her doubts would have multiplied.

She hurried downstairs to the library, wishing to be seated there when her visitor was announced. She looked round her favourite room, checking all was as it should be and that Edward had not left any books untidily on the tables. Satisfied, she resumed her study of the list of questions she wished to ask the man applying for the position as tutor, and companion, to her seven-year-old son.

Sarah straightened at the sound of footsteps in the passage-way outside. Mrs Thomas, the housekeeper, appeared in the open doorway.

'Captain Mayhew is here to see you, madam.'

'Thank you, Mrs Thomas, please show him in.'

Her heart thudded uncomfortably and she deeply regretted having allowed her mother-in-law, Lady Hepworth, to persuade her to take this action. Interviewing strange gentle-men was something to which she was not accustomed. Since the demise of her dear husband, Jonathan, six years previously, she had lived a sheltered life and met few men of any sort. Indeed she employed no males in her house at all. Sarah stood up and smoothed the skirts of her plain blue morning-dress. She could hear heavy footsteps following Mrs Thomas.

'Captain Mayhew, madam.' Sarah's mouth rounded and her jaw dropped.

'Good afternoon, Mrs Haverstock, Oliver Mayhew at your service.' The tall, dark, grey eyed soldier bowed, but didn't offer his hand.

She recovered her wits. She had not considered that Captain Mayhew might be so formidable. But why would such a man wish to take a position more suited to a scholar than a man of action?

'I am pleased to make your acquaintance, Captain. Thank you for agreeing to travel down to see me.' Sarah indicated one of the upright, wooden chairs. 'Would you please be seated? Can I send for some refreshments?'

He bowed again. 'No, thank you, madam.' He waited until his hostess had resumed her place then expertly flicked aside the back of his navy blue coat and folded his considerable length onto the chair.

Sarah noted, crossly, that he was more at ease than she was. This man was totally unsuitable, not the sort of person she had in mind to have sole charge of her darling son. Certain she was not going to offer Captain Mayhew the position, the interview immediately became irrelevant. Relaxing at this comforting thought, she smiled for the first time.

Up to that point Oliver Mayhew had seen and dismissed Sarah as a woman of medium height, reasonable figure and ordinary features. He had already decided to refuse the job when it was offered; there was nothing to interest him at Rowley Court. It had been a wasted journey.

Then Sarah's smile transformed her face from common-place to breathtaking. Her eyes, he now realized, were an extraordinary mix of emerald green and darkest brown and he fell into their intriguing depths. He swallowed, twice, and forced his limbs to relax, angry that such an experienced man as he, had allowed himself to be floored by a pair of what had to be the finest eyes in England.

'Are you feeling quite well, Captain Mayhew? You have gone quite pale. I will order some refreshments. I expect you are fatigued after your long journey.' She stood up and pulled the bell-strap. Her actions allowed him time to recover.

'Thank you, ma'am, that would be most kind.' He hid his amusement well. Had she forgotten he was a veteran of the Peninsular? The thirty-five miles from town was a mere bagatelle.

Sarah ordered a cold collation to be prepared and served immediately in the small dining-room. She resumed her seat, and folded her hands tightly round her list, smiled again and Oliver swallowed again.

'Now, Captain, I have a list of questions I wish to ask you. Are you feeling well enough to commence?'

He nodded, his expression bland. 'Yes, Mrs Haverstock, I am quite ready. What would you like to know?'

'Firstly, why should an ex-officer, from a noble family, wish to take employment as a tutor in such a countrified establishment as this?'

'My birth, as you rightly point out, is impeccable but as a third son, my expectations are nil. My family has an impressive pedigree but there are no funds to go with it.' Absently he leant down and flicked a speck of dust from his polished Hessians. He raised his head, his strange blue-grey eyes met hers and he smiled. 'Therefore, as Bonaparte is now on Elba, I must find paid employment or starve. Next question?'

Sarah's hands trembled and she felt her colour rise. This would not do! She was a mature woman of eight and twenty, a widow with a seven-year-old son, not a moonstruck debutante to be taken in by a handsome soldier with a devastating smile.

'My next question, Captain Mayhew, is how do you regard the use of corporal punishment?'

Oliver sat up. 'Not necessary. I totally disagree with its use, for any child.'

'Good, then on that we can agree.' A maid-servant arrived to inform them that his meal was ready. Sarah rose gracefully. 'Please go and eat, Captain. Whilst you do so I will fetch Edward. It is imperative that you are able to establish a rapport with him. As I explained, in my letter, I am quite capable of supplying him with a suitable education but what Edward needs is masculine guidance; he is spending too much time with my outside servants.'

Oliver understood. 'And he is hearing, and doing, things you consider unsuitable?'

'Exactly. I need a gentleman who can teach him the things he will need to know when he is ready to take his rightful place in the world.'

'Naturally you do, ma'am. As you know I am well educated, speak three languages, and am competent in the classics and mathematics. The natural sciences and botany are a particular interest of mine.' Oliver considered this last a master-stroke. Jonathan Haverstock had been recognized internationally as a botanist of repute and, at the time of his death, he had been compiling a record of the flora and fauna of Surrey.

Sarah nodded; maybe Captain Mayhew was not as incompatible as she had first thought. They parted, he to follow the maidservant to the small dining-room, she to run upstairs to her son's domain on the second floor.

The small olive-skinned boy looked up eagerly as his mother entered the room.

'What is he like, Mama?'

Sarah hesitated before answering. 'Captain Mayhew is tall, and lean, and well over six feet, I would say. He has strange blue-grey eyes and dark hair, which he has long, to his collar.'

'What is he wearing? Is he bang up?'

Sarah shuddered at his language but refrained from comment.

'His jacket is dark blue and well cut, but not, I think, from

10

Weston, for it does not fit snugly enough. His cravat is simple, his waistcoat plain, but I misremember the colour.'

Edward smiled. 'I like the cut of his jib, Mama. Is he fierce or friendly? Does he like animals? Would he like Rags?'

She laughed. 'Enough questions, Edward, my dear; come and meet him for yourself. You know I will not employ him if you do not wish me to. I want you to be happy in his company.'

'If he likes animals and does not shout at me, I will be happy, Mama. I am going to fetch Rags; Captain Mayhew must meet him as well.'

His mother shuddered. 'If you insist, my love. Has your dog had a bath recently?' The last time she had seen the enormous, hairy animal, he had been liberally smeared with stable dung.

'Of course he has. Jack and I washed him under the pump. I think he gets smelly just because he so loves being washed.'

Edward clattered ahead, down the uncarpeted backstairs, and dashed out into the yard to find his constant companion.

'Rags, come here boy.' The dog came bounding round the corner to skid to an ungainly halt, all paws and lolling tongue, in front of his young master. Edward dropped to his knees and hugged him. 'Good boy! Well done!'

'Get up from the dirt, please, darling,' Sarah gently remonstrated. Edward ignored her. He sat back on his heels and scrutinized his pet.

'You look very smart. Has Jack been grooming you this morning?' In answer the dog, his huge grey and black head on a level with the boy's, smothered Edward's face with wet, sloppy licks.

Sarah had seen enough. 'Edward, get up now. Do as I bid you, please.'

Her son grinned over his shoulder, not moving. 'Does he not look smart, Mama? I believe Captain Mayhew will be impressed.'

11

'He will not be impressed with you, Edward, if you are covered in mud and dog hairs.'

Finally he stood up, glancing cursorily down at his tweed breeches and wrinkled stockings.

'I am not really dirty; it is only dust, it will brush off easily.' He banged ineffectually at the mud.

'Come here, you silly boy, let me do it.' Sarah, with the ease of long practice, removed the grime and dog hairs and straightened his jacket. 'There, that is much better.'

A loud yelp startled her. She laughed. 'And yes, you look very smart too, Rags.' The dog waved his plumy tail and his liquid brown eyes radiated his devotion. 'We must go in, Edward. You had best hold his collar. Remember what happened last time he came in and met Tabby on the stairs.'

Edward giggled. 'Cats should stay in the kitchen. It served her right for being where she shouldn't be.'

'Poor thing, she stayed hidden on top of the wardrobe in my bedchamber for the rest of the day.'

'I bet Rags would chase a burglar too, Mama, if we had one. I wish you would allow him to sleep in my room with me. He gets so lonely in the stable.'

'Nonsense, my love. He is not a house pet and we agreed when you got him that he should live outside.'

The dog walked placidly beside Edward, sniffing the unaccustomed smells with delight, hoping he might meet another intruder to chase. The incongruous trio entered the study to find the captain already in occupation.

'Good God! Whatever is that object?' His astonishment had overcome his good manners.

The dog, recognizing the reference to himself, bounced forward taking Edward with him. The resulting heap of arms and legs entangled on the carpet immediately dispensed with ceremony. Winded, but laughing, Oliver extracted himself from the pile and stood up, taking Edward with him.

'Are you hurt, lad? Did I tread on you?'

Edward was so relieved the captain was not enraged that he had temporarily forgotten his own woes. Now, however, the pain from his squashed hand overwhelmed him. His chin wobbled and bravely he choked back his tears.

'My hand is a little hurt, sir, but otherwise I received no injury, thank you for asking.'

When Sarah had watched the intimidating stranger vanish under a mêlée of dog and child she had not known whether to smile or frown. But on hearing her son's tearful admission that he was in pain she rushed forward and scooped him up, and he allowed himself to be petted and cosseted.

'There, there, my darling, let me see. You are so very brave.' As Sarah was kissing the injured appendage she happened to glance up and found Captain Mayhew watching her performance with distaste. Embarrassed to be seen as such a doting mother she, to her son's relief, released him.

Edward rubbed his well kissed hand on his breeches and grinned at Oliver.

'Do you not think my dog is splendid, Captain Mayhew?' The miscreant, now calmly seated at the captain's feet, thumped his tail in agreement.

Oliver smiled. 'He is an excellent dog, Edward, but his place is outside, not in the house.'

The boy coloured. 'Yes, sir. I will take him out at once.'

Sarah watched as her son grabbed the dog's collar and hurried off without a murmur of protest.

'I must apologize to you, Captain Mayhew. The dog is not normally permitted indoors, but Edward begged for my permission to introduce him to you.'

'And you succumbed to his pleas?' His reply was mild but Sarah knew he thought her a foolish and overindulgent parent.

'Yes, I am afraid I did.' She moved towards a chair and sat down, gesturing to the captain to do likewise, giving herself time to become more composed. 'I should be more firm with him, I am aware of that. It is not good to spoil him but, you must remember, he is all I have; and he is such a sweet boy, he never takes advantage of my partiality.'

Oliver leant forward, fixing Sarah with his stare.

'If I am to become Edward's tutor, and companion, Mrs Haverstock, such pampering will have to cease. I would expect full control of the boy he must not be permitted to run to you for comfort and protection.'

She stiffened. How dare he suggest she was an inadequate mother? She drew breath to give a sharp set-down then paused, realizing he had made a valid point.

'I will be happy to place Edward's education in your hands, Captain Mayhew, and would not dream of interfering with that process, any more than my son would dream of disobeying your instructions.' Oliver sat back, a small smile of satisfaction flickering across his austere features.

'However,' Sarah continued, 'I am his mother, and legal guardian, and you will be in my employ. I hope you appreciate what that means?'

He hid his anger. 'Of course, madam.'

'I am glad that we understand each other, Captain. Now I believe we can move on to the details. You will be accommodated in the Dower House; it would not be fitting for you to reside here. I will provide the necessary staff to take care of you, of course.'

'Forgive me, ma'am, I would prefer to appoint my own men, if you have no objection?'

'No, of course not. It will actually be more convenient for you to do so. It is also my intention to provide you with two hacks. My son is an excellent horseman and I wish him to ride out frequently.' Sarah stood up, thus terminating the interview, and rang the bell. 'I suggest a three-month trial; if after this, we are both satisfied, I will make the appointment permanent. Your salary will be as stated in the letter. Do you have any further questions, Captain?'

14

He bowed, his expression open, but his eyes narrowed. 'None, I believe you have covered everything to perfection. When do you wish me to start?'

'Can you be here by the first of May? This will allow two weeks for the Dower House to be refurbished.'

'That will be acceptable. I have only to resign my commission at Horse Guards and then I am free of obligations.'

Sarah examined the enigmatic man standing opposite and came to a decision. 'It might be best if you selected your own mounts, Captain. There is a fine stud a few miles south of here.'

He bowed again. 'Thank you, Mrs Haverstock. I will visit the place on my return. Now, if you will excuse me, I will take my leave.'

Sarah didn't offer her hand. 'Until May then, Captain? I will expect to see an education schedule for Edward on your return. Will that be convenient?'

'I will have it, of course. Good day to you, Mrs Haverstock.'

He followed the maid-servant, who bobbed him a nervous curtsy. Sarah watched his back, ramrod straight, disappear down the passageway. Her knees, unexpectedly, refused to hold her upright and she was forced to grab the back of a chair for support. What had possessed her to appoint Captain Mayhew? He was the antithesis of everything she had envisaged for Edward's mentor. She sank into the chair and dropped her head into her hands. She heard running footsteps approaching the study, and not wishing her son to see her so overset, dried her eyes, and pinched her cheeks to restore some much-needed colour.

'Mama, Captain Mayhew says he is to be my tutor. I am so glad. He is a capital fellow, I was so afraid you would appoint a flat.'

'Edward, you must not use such language, it is quite unsuitable.'

He grinned, unrepentant. 'Sorry, Mama. Rags is happy too.

15

Captain Mayhew promised that he would teach me how to box, and use a pistol. When is he starting, I hope it is soon?'

'In two weeks, darling,' she replied faintly, her unease returning at her son's mention of pugilism and guns. Captain Mayhew was totally unsuited for the task to which she had appointed him and whatever his qualifications, and however much her son and his dog wished him to stay, she was determined that, after the three months, the man would leave Rowley Court and someone more suitable would be found.

Chapter Two

'CAPTAIN Mayhew's men have arrived, Mama,' Edward shouted when he saw his mother talking to Jack, the stable boy, in the drive.

'Please do not shout at me, Edward, it is extremely bad manners,' Sarah said, as her son slithered to a halt beside her.

'You would not have heard me, if I had not shouted.'

Sarah sighed. 'Then you should have waited until you were near enough to speak, my love.' She ruffled his hair, stuck damply to his grubby forehead. 'Would you like to walk down to the Dower House, Edward? I have not fully inspected it since the repairs were completed.'

'Yes, please, Rags will enjoy the walk and he needs to meet the new men; you know how he growls at strangers.'

'Indeed I do, my dear. And I do not believe the new curate will ever forget the experience, either.'

Sarah, Edward, and his shadow Rags, a curious mix of wolfhound and village mongrel, strolled off towards what was to be the residence of Captain Mayhew in two days' time. The one-mile walk took them through Home Wood, a charming arrangement of silver birch, hazelnut, and hornbeam, verdant with fresh spring growth and carpeted with bluebells.

Suddenly the dog stopped and his hackles rose forming a fearsome ruff around his head. He curled back his lips and snarled, baring his fangs. Sarah froze and instinctively pulled

Edward into her side.

She whispered to the rigid animal. 'What is it, Rags? What can you smell?' The dog remained at their side, protectively, staring at the enemy invisible to human eyes, lurking in the undergrowth ahead. Edward pressed closer to his mother, she could feel him trembling.

Sarah squeezed her son's shoulder. 'We will return to the house, Edward. It is possible there is a poacher in the wood.' Still holding her son she turned, exposing their backs to the intruder. 'Come along darling, I am sure whoever it is will be as relieved as we are not be forced to meet face-to-face.'

She hurried back down the dappled path, glancing nervously from side to side. The trees, which moments before had been a delightful harbinger of summer, now seemed full of danger and shadows. They were almost running when they emerged into the sunlight.

Edward stopped. 'Rags is still in there, Mama. We cannot leave him; I could not bear anything bad to happen to him.'

'Call him, Edward. I am sure he will come back now that you are in no danger.'

Edward drew breath to shout but his call was unnecessary for the dog loped out of the wood, the epitome of canine docility. Rags pushed his nose into Edward's face and his long pink tongue cleaned up the tears. For once Sarah didn't protest, instead she patted the hairy head with gratitude.

'Good dog, Rags. What did you see in there?'

'I told you he would be good with a burglar, Mama,' her son said, his fear quickly forgotten.

'And you were quite right, darling. Now, come along, I wish to have the wood investigated. I will send some of the grooms.'

'Who do you think it was, Mama?'

'Poachers, Edward. I believe Lord Hepworth mentioned that there has been an influx of vagrants recently; probably they are displaced men who once fought in the wars.'

Edward smiled and finally released his vice-like grip on his mother's hand. 'If they are ex-soldiers, Mama, then they would not wish us any harm, would they?'

'No, love, I am sure they were merely searching for something to eat, but it is better if they are discouraged from poaching in our woods.' Sarah fixed a smile to her pale face and expertly turned the conversation to a less worrying subject.

The men she sent to investigate found nothing untoward in the Home Wood, or anywhere else. Sarah believed that whoever might have been hiding there had, sensibly, retreated to less hazardous hunting grounds.

Edward did not mention a visit to the Dower House again and made no protest when his mother restricted his freedom to the immediate environs of Rowley Court. That Jack, the thirteen-year-old stable lad, was now permanently at his side, he took as fortuitous, which suited Sarah well.

She had swung from rather dreading the arrival of Edward's tutor to eagerly anticipating the day. Whatever her personal reservations about Captain Mayhew she knew she would feel safer when he was living nearby.

The first of May dawned bright and sunny, as befitted the official start of summer. Sarah had intended to take Edward to the village green to watch the maypole dancing but instead she sent him with Jack, his nurse-maid Sally, two stout grooms and his dog. If Edward thought this strange he did not comment; as long as he got to see the festivities he cared little who accompanied him. Rags was firmly attached to a piece of rope, which Jack had been instructed to keep hold of at all times.

Satisfied that she had provided her son was sufficient protection Sarah was able to turn her mind to the forthcoming meeting with Captain Mayhew. She had been informed that he was already in residence; he had arrived the previous night. So she waited in the library for his arrival. However it was not of lesson plans and leisure schedules that she wished to talk.

Sarah paced the carpet, her pretty dimity morning-gown swirling round her slippered feet at every impatient turn. She patted her neatly coiffured hair and wondered if she should have donned a cap; after all she was a widow, and in polite society a cap would be *de rigueur*. She sniffed inelegantly at the thought. She was an independent, wealthy woman and, expected or not, she would not wear such silly headgear.

She heard, at last, the sound of masculine footsteps, preceded by the lighter footfalls of a housemaid. She turned to face the door, her face becomingly flushed by her exertions, her huge hazel eyes sparkling with eagerness.

The maid announced the captain and he strode in. Before he could acknowledge his employer she stepped forward to greet him.

'Captain Mayhew, welcome indeed. I have been counting the hours to your arrival. Come in, I have much to discuss with you.'

Oliver was somewhat disconcerted by her enthusiasm. They had not parted on good terms, what could have happened in his absence to turn his employer from haughty lady to eager friend? Whatever it was, it could only be of benefit to his plans.

'Good morning, Mrs Haverstock. I hope I find you well?' His polite enquiry hung in the space between them. Belatedly Sarah realized she had allowed her anxiety to overcome her natural good manners.

She flushed and, closing the gap, held out her hand. 'Good morning, Captain, I am well, thank you. I hope you have found everything as it should be at the Dower House?'

Oliver hesitated, and then took the proffered hand. He held it lightly, but still a wave of heat pulsed through his body. He half bowed and, dismayed by his reaction, released her instantly and stepped away.

'Everything is splendid, thank you ma'am,' he said gruffly. He cleared his throat. 'I have Edward's timetable here, as promised.' He reached into his jacket and removed a bulky packet of closely written papers.

'Good, good.' Sarah took the packet and tossed it on to a nearby table. 'I will study it later, thank you. Please be seated, I have something of far greater import to discuss.'

They selected chairs as far apart as the restrictions of the room allowed. She waited for him to settle then began to explain her concerns. 'Two days ago Edward and I decided to walk through the wood to inspect the Dower House and introduce ourselves to your men.' She paused, closing her eyes for a second, as she relived the experience. He had her full attention now.

'Go on, ma'am,' he prompted.

She shivered and shook her head hoping to dispel the sick feeling her thoughts had engendered.

'We were in the deepest part, where the thickets are dense and the trees overhang the path, do you know where I mean, Captain?'

He nodded. The spot she mentioned was as far from either house as it was possible to be.

'Rags heard something, or someone, and stopped and growled ferociously. I have never seen him so angry; he knew we were in danger and was protecting us.'

'Did you see anything, ma'am?'

'No, but I could feel malevolent eyes staring at us from the darkness ahead.'

'What happened next?'

'We turned back and I sent some of my men to search, but they found nothing. Whoever had been there was long gone.'

'There are, I heard, vagrants in the vicinity; it was most likely a couple of them looking for rabbits, nothing to alarm yourself over, Mrs Haverstock.'

The patronizing dismissal of her fears incensed her. He had not been there, he had not breathed in the evil that had permeated the wood that day. She pushed her shoulders back, her informality gone.

'Whatever your opinion of the matter, Captain Mayhew, I must insist that your men patrol the woods on a regular basis. Neither will you permit Edward to venture there alone, at any time.'

He clenched his teeth, his face expressionless. 'Of course, madam, I fully understand. Do you wish to discuss my proposals for Edward?'

Sarah glanced at the discarded papers. 'I will study them later, Captain Mayhew. If you could attend me here, at four this afternoon, I will give you my opinion then.' She stood. 'Edward's waiting in the schoolroom; I will have you conducted there.'

She rang the bell and they stood in frosty silence until the maid arrived in answer to the summons.

'Please take Captain Mayhew to the schoolroom.' Sarah didn't wait for him to exit; she turned her back and walked over to stare out of the library window. Her incivility was noted.

'Come this way, sir, if you please.'

The door closed allowing Sarah to give full rein to her anger. She had always prided herself on her calm and patient demeanour but that man would infuriate a saint. She needed to vent her spleen on something and snatched up an inoffensive copy of her latest novel and threw it, with more haste than accuracy, at the door. The resulting crash relieved her anger but destroyed the book.

Immediately regretting her unaccustomed burst of fury she ran across and picked it up.

'Oh dear! It is quite ruined and I have not read it yet,' she exclaimed out loud. 'Well, it serves me right. I should know better than to throw books at my age'

Hastily she collected the scattered pages and thrust them into the drawer of the handsome oak desk that dominated the centre of the library. Next she retrieved the papers Captain Mayhew had handed her. Reading them would be therapeutic and allow her jangled sensibilities time to recover.

After half an hour of interminable detail she admitted defeat. She had been hoist with her own petard; Captain Mayhew had left no minute of the day unaccounted for. When she had demanded a work schedule she had expected a page or two of details, a broad outline of the curriculum he intended to follow, but not this. What she had been given would take her several hours to read.

Thoughtfully she placed the pile of, mostly unread, paper on the desk and weighted it down with the large painted stone Edward had decorated for her name-day gift. She had underestimated the captain, for his response to her demand had shown subtlety and a sense of humour. She recalled his introduction to Edward's dog; he had laughed and shown no sign of annoyance.

Her son would enjoy the company of a man who laughed easily. She smiled at the thought, knowing the captain would need not only the ability to see humour, where others might not, but also the patience of Job, if he was not to become exasperated with Edward. Even she was not blind to the fact that her son was headstrong.

Sarah met with her Estate Manager, discussed the planting of the potager with her head gardener, and wrote a letter to her sister, who had recently produced a long-awaited son for her doting spouse, Sir James Humphrey of Thrandeston, Norfolk. Of Edward, and his tutor, she saw nothing, but trusting he was in safe hands she felt no need to worry.

After eating a light luncheon in the sunny, south facing, breakfast room she decided that she needed some fresh air and exercise. It was far too pleasant a day to languish inside.

Beth, her personal maid, was summoned and assisted her mistress to change from her morning-dress into a dashing, military style, riding habit.

The severity of the cut emphasized Sarah's curves and the green reflected the colour in her eyes. Although she did not visit Town in season, Sarah was no dowd. She kept in touch with current trends and, selecting the less extreme designs from *La Belle Assemble*, had them made up by a mantua-maker, Mrs Andrews, from the nearby town of Market Camden.

The floating, transparent gauze creations that were all the rage were not for her. However she had adopted the high waistline and scooped neck, finding such garments comfortable. Contrary to all the dictates of society, she refused to wear a corset, believing freedom to breathe more important than fashion.

Her mount, a pretty chestnut mare who answered to the sobriquet of 'Smoke', was patiently awaiting her arrival, at the foot of the white marble steps, her head held by Jack.

'Good afternoon, Smoke is looking well.'

'Thank you, madam.' Jack handed her up and placed her foot in the single stirrup. The young groom, William, who was to accompany her on a handsome bay hunter, mounted also.

Skirts adjusted, Sarah gathered up the reins and Jack released the horse.

'I am going to ride over to Hepworth House, William, across the park – the horses can stretch their legs there – and then we will take the lane through the village.'

'Very well, madam.' If William considered it strange they were not taking the shorter route through Home Wood, he kept the thought to himself.

Sarah trotted up the drive happy, as always, to be visiting her mother-in-law. Lady Hepworth had remarried after the death of her first husband, Henry Haverstock, and now had a brood of hopeful daughters. Lord Hepworth, an amiable man, loved his step-grandson as dearly as his own children.

A groom hurried round to hold Smoke. William knew better than to offer to assist his mistress to dismount. The butler opened the door as Sarah arrived at the top step, her feathered tricorn hat held in one hand, her skirts gathered up in the other.

'Her Ladyship is in the orangery, madam.'

'Thank you, I shall find my own way,' Sarah replied, glad ceremony was not stood on here, any more than it was at Rowley Court.

Her mother-in-law beamed as Sarah entered.

'Welcome, my dear. I was hoping you would come over today and tell me how your Captain Mayhew is settling in.'

Sarah bent over and kissed the proffered cheek, the soft flesh warm under her lips.

'You are looking well, Harriet, that shade of lavender suits you.'

Lady Hepworth smoothed the silk between her plump fingers.

'It is a pretty colour, is it not? Though I am not at all certain this new high-waisted look is suitable for a woman of my size and years.'

'Nonsense, you look lovely. You are neither old, nor fat, so do not fish for compliments.'

Harriet chuckled. 'I am eight and forty, and well you know it Sarah, and seriously overweight.'

'You are a little plump, I agree, and indeed, who would not be after producing five children?' She settled herself comfortably on the deep cushioned armchair. 'How are the girls?'

'Blooming, as always. Miss Briggs has taken them on a nature walk to the bluebell woods, so we have time for a comfortable coze.'

It was after five when Sarah left Hepworth House. She had completely forgotten she had arranged to meet with Captain Mayhew at four o'clock that afternoon.

Chapter Three

SARAH drew rein outside her front door. She dismounted and smiled her thanks to her groom and patted her horse's sweat-stained neck. The time was now a little after six o'clock and she recalled, from her son's itinerary, that he should now be in the schoolroom preparing his lessons for the following day.

As she ran up the steps two thoughts occurred to her simultaneously, neither of them happy. The first that she had sent the captain up to the schoolroom, after their brief meeting, and her son would not have been there because she had allowed him to go to the village to visit the May fair. The second that she had ordered him to attend her at four o'clock and she had also been absent.

With a sinking heart she entered the hall. Mrs Thomas, the housekeeper, bustled up to meet her.

'Madam, Captain Mayhew has been waiting to see you in the library for the past two hours. He is still there. I've offered him refreshments but he has refused.'

'Would you send in my sincere apologies for wasting his time? I will see him tomorrow after breakfast.' Sarah hurried up the stairs and along the wide, light-filled passageway to her bedchamber. She had no desire to be accosted by the man she had left kicking his heels for over two hours.

At her chamber door she paused, undecided, then turned and walked briskly back. She had been unpardonably rude and it was her duty to make her apologies; Captain Mayhew may be her employee but he deserved to be treated with respect.

She reached the spacious marble-tiled hall the same time as the captain. For a moment they stood, eyes locked, frozen, on her part by embarrassment and on his by anger.

Sarah broke the silence.

'Captain Mayhew, I am so sorry. I have no excuse for my incivility. I realize that twice today I have misdirected you.'

The hardness of his jaw relaxed. He nodded, stiffly. 'After your encounter with poachers, madam, I was naturally becoming worried by your continued absence.'

'Thank you for your concern. I can only apologise again, Captain. There was no problem, I am afraid I had completely forgotten that I had arranged to meet with you.' She smiled, warmed by his concern for her welfare. It was years since anyone had taken note of her whereabouts.

She laughed, the unexpected sound disarming him. Oliver smiled back and, for the first time Sarah felt the impact of his charm. Her mouth went dry and she felt a peculiar sensation deep inside her. She took an involuntary step back and trod clumsily on the hem of her skirt and stumbled. An iron-hard hand shot out and caught her. His touch burnt through the sleeve of her habit.

Oliver snatched his hand back and moved away, his expression unreadable.

'If you will excuse me, madam, I have left my charge too long unattended.'

Sarah believed that the oblique reference to her lack of manners was uncalled for.

'Of course, Captain. I will see you tomorrow; will ten o'clock be convenient?'

He nodded and without further speech, stepped around her and, taking the stairs two at a time, disappeared towards the schoolroom. He left Sarah in no doubt he was as eager as she to finish the encounter. Suddenly exhausted she retraced her steps and returned to her room where Beth was waiting with a restorative bath and change of raiment.

It was her custom to oversee Edward's night-time preparations herself but she was reluctant to go up to his rooms, not sure exactly when his tutor would consider his duties completed. She wished that she had studied his timetable more carefully. She decided to send Beth to fetch her son.

Her abigail returned immediately. 'Master Edward is asleep, madam. Only Sally is up there straightening the schoolroom. Do you wish me to wake him?'

Sarah glanced at the large clock ticking loudly in the corner of the drawing-room. 'Good heavens, it is scarcely seven o'clock! I can never persuade Edward into bed much before nine. I hope he is not unwell.' Worried that her son had retired without waiting to see her she determined to go to the nursery. If he was running a fever she should have been informed. Not sure whether she was angry or concerned Sarah flew up the narrow nursery stairs.

Sally paused in her duties, a pile of books in her ample arms. 'Madam, is there something amiss?'

'Indeed, I hope not. I wish to know why Master Edward is asleep so early? Is he ailing?' His father had succumbed to congestion in the lungs, which had started, innocently enough, as a slight fever and an aching in the bones. She would not let the same thing happen to his son.

The nurse-maid grinned. 'No, madam, Master Edward is fit as a flea, bless him. But was that tired after his morning at the fair, and an afternoon of lessons, that Captain Mayhew said he should go straight to bed after tea.'

Sarah bristled. How dare he interfere with her son's routine? Had she not made it clear where his boundaries were? However it was not poor Sally's fault. She forced herself to smile.

'And he went without a protest?' The girl nodded. 'Captain

Mayhew is obviously going to be a good influence on Master Edward.'

'Yes, madam, the little lad did not stop talking about the captain all through his tea and bath.'

Sarah's smile became even more fixed. 'Excellent. It is good that they have taken a liking to each other so soon. I am going to look in on Edward before I depart. Goodnight, Sally.'

Sarah slipped quietly into her son's room; the evening sun filtered through the drawn curtains making it easy for her to see Edward's sleeping form. She bent down and kissed his forehead and he mumbled in his sleep and rolled over on his side.

It was then she noticed that his favourite toy, a dilapidated stuffed animal that vaguely resembled a dog, was missing from its customary place upon his pillow. He resolutely refused to sleep without it, but here he was, resting peacefully, no toy in view. Angrily she straightened. It was no doubt Captain Mayhew who had interfered again and confiscated her son's precious bedtime comforter.

Had her beloved child cried himself silently to sleep lonely and too scared to ask for its return? The miserable man had only been here a day and already her son was being taken from her. The curate, from the village, was a well educated and harmless young man; she should have arranged for Edward to attend lessons with him. It was small comfort to her that the captain's appointment was for only three months.

Thoughtfully she headed for the drawing-room. Tears prickled behind her eyelids and her throat constricted. By the time the probationary period was over, and she could dismiss him, her son would be so attached to his tutor that the departure would break his heart. Edward did not remember his father – he had been too young – but he was now at an age when such a loss could cause irreparable harm.

Tortured by indecision and conflicting emotions Sarah was too fraught to sit at her embroidery frame or read a novel. She had ordered supper to be served at nine, so had more than an hour to spare. She would go out for a walk, it was light still, and with a thick cloak she would be warm enough.

The grass was damp underfoot and she was glad she had taken the time to change into stout half-boots. She could hear the grooms settling the horses in the stables so decided not to visit there. Instead, she turned towards the artificial lake constructed by the previous owners from the damming of two small brooks that ran across the park. Its surface rippled invitingly, pink and gold, as the sun sank slowly behind the bordering trees. She stepped out briskly, knowing she could easily complete the walk before full darkness overtook the park.

Sarah stood entranced at the lake side watching the sun vanish, rolling up its fiery skirts as it disappeared behind the trees. The water rippled metal-grey in the twilight and the stange colour reminded her of eyes she would much prefer to forget.

A chill breeze blew from the water and Sarah gathered up her cloak, glad she had had the foresight to put it on. A flicker of movement in a bank of rhododendrons, their cheerful blaze of blossom dulled in the fading light, attracted her attention.

Had she imagined it? She blinked and stared into them but could see nothing untoward. Only partially reassured, she shivered and reached behind her head to pull up the voluminous hood of her cloak. As she did so she heard a sound, somewhere between a cough and a bang, and felt a stinging pain in the back of her head. Thinking that she had been stung by an early bee, trapped unwittingly in the folds of material, she flung her hood back and the cold air burned her scalp unpleasantly.

She was beginning to feel rather sick; was she experiencing an unexpected reaction to the bee venom? She turned to retrace her steps but the outline of the house flickered and wavered in front of her. She felt as though she was looking at it through the wrong end of a spyglass. A roaring noise filled her ears and she knew nothing more. Softly, full darkness enveloped the park and Sarah lay almost invisible in her dark cloak, spread-eagled on the ground.

Oliver was aroused from his perusal of the next day's lessons by a furious knocking. Not waiting for his man to appear, he surged out into the flagged hallway and unbolted the door. Jack did not wait for him to enquire the reason for his visit.

'Captain, sir, madam is missing. She went out for a stroll before supper, two hours since, and she has not returned. The house is in an uproar. Could you come and organise a proper search?'

'Wait there, lad; I will be with you in a moment.' He turned and ran down the passage. 'Jenkins, Peters, here, now, and bring lanterns with you.' He shrugged into his coat, for once careless of his appearance. Mrs Haverstock had obviously suffered some mishap and needed his assistance. His two men, who had once served with him, appeared carrying lanterns already ablaze with light.

'Something up then, Captain?' Jenkins asked.

'Mrs Haverstock is missing somewhere in the park. We are going to find her.' He strode off, no stranger to the dark, his eyes adjusting instantly; he had no need to rely on lanterns to light his path. The faint shimmer supplied by the new moon was enough. Jack trotted along beside him.

Oliver barked questions as they travelled. 'Where was your mistress going?'

'She did not say, sir.'

'Where have they searched so far?'

'I'm not sure, sir. They are running about in all directions in a panic.'

Oliver's face was grim. A lake-side stroll, in the gathering dark, was the height of foolishness. It should surely have been completed in an hour? He ground his teeth, pushing aside the image that filled his head, of a shapeless female form floating, face down, in the water of the lake. He broke into a rapid jog, his men keeping pace, their lanterns bobbing merrily, but Jack fell back, unable to keep up.

The Court appeared to be surrounded by a small swarm of angry yellow bees, as the grooms and gardeners, routed out by Mrs Thomas, searched haphazardly amongst the flowerbeds and shrubberies. Within moments of his arrival the captain had marshalled his troops and turned chaos into calm.

'Jenkins, take those three men and walk abreast, west, towards the gate. Peters, do the same, but walk north. You, Tom Coachman, take your men east. I will go south, towards the lake.' Belatedly he remembered Edward's dog. 'Jack, fetch Rags; he has a better chance of finding his mistress than we do.'

The dog arrived before Jack, his whole body alive with the joy of meeting his new friend again. Oliver dropped to his haunches and took the dog's head between his hands. 'Your mistress is missing, Rags. Can you find her for us?' The dog licked his face and yelped. 'I do believe the animal understands.'

'That he does, sir, every word. A very intelligent dog is that,' Jack told him proudly.

'Off you go, boy, find her – find her!' The captain released his hold and sprung to his feet. The dog vanished into the darkness, nose to the ground as though already following a scent.

The men, lanterns aloft, ran behind but stayed a yard apart as instructed by the captain. Oliver pounded after Rags. He had a bad feeling about this and his instincts rarely let him down.

He had the lake in sight when the dog started howling and, as one, the line swung sideways and ran towards the noise. Oliver reached Sarah's unconscious form first. He flung himself down and pushing the excited dog aside, expertly placed his fingers under her jawbone, searching for a pulse. A sigh whistled through his teeth. It was strong and even. Whatever ill had befallen her, she was not, at that moment, in mortal danger.

'Bring the light closer,' he ordered. The lanterns obediently appeared above his head. He reached out and unhooked one from its pole. Starting at her feet he moved the light along, searching for any injury.

The light halted over Sarah's head and illuminated her ghastly pallor. Jack swallowed a sob of distress. Oliver glanced over his shoulder and smiled at the boy.

'Steady, lad, your mistress is not dying. She has a steady pulse.'

'But she is so white, sir, and still.'

'I know, Jack, but I promise it is not as bad as it looks.' He handed the lantern back to its owner. He needed his hands free to continue the examination. 'Keep the light still, and hold it behind my head.' The lantern ceased bobbing and the golden glow pooled over Sarah's unconscious form. He carefully ran his fingers under her head and his stomach lurched as he felt a tell-tale, sticky wetness.

For a moment he remained still, realizing that when he withdrew his hands, his audience would see the evidence.

'Untie my stock, Jack.' The boy fumbled, and then the cloth was free. 'I need it folded into a pad, if you can; then hand it to me.' By now all had guessed that the injury was to Mrs Haverstock's head.

The captain removed one hand, still cradling her head in the other, and Jack placed the makeshift bandage in it. Then, with the efficiency of long practice, he slipped the wad of folded cloth behind her head and pressed it over the wound he could feel under his fingers.

'Good, that will suffice for the moment. Peters and Jenkins, are you with me?' The men stepped forward into the light.

'Peters, here, hold this light above Mrs Haverstock's head.' When he was sure the bandage was held securely in place Oliver slid one arm under Sarah's shoulders, the other behind her knees. 'Jenkins, steady me as I stand.' He swayed back and, in one sure move, regained his feet, holding his burden safely to his chest.

'Jack, ran back and alert the house. I will require boiled water and clean cloths ready.'

'Yes, sir.' The boy raced away as directed, leaving the other searchers to encircle Captain Mayhew and escort him back across the park.

Without giving the appearance of haste, Oliver walked fast, knowing the longer the woman who lay limp and cold within his arms was outside in the chill dark, the higher the risk of her succumbing to infection and fever.

Mrs Thomas was waiting anxiously at the open door. 'Bring the mistress straight up, sir; her maid has everything prepared.'

Oliver mounted the stairs, Peters still holding the makeshift bandage, and followed the housekeeper into a bedchamber. He was glad to see a log fire blazing in the hearth. Beth and two maids were waiting, ready to minister as required. The bowls of steaming water and clean linen strips lay on a small side table.

The bed covers had been folded back so he placed her there. He snatched up a strip of cloth and tied it tightly around her head, then stood back. He had done all he could for the moment, it was up to her women to do the next part.

'Get your mistress out of these wet garments and into something warm. Are there hot bricks in the bed?'

'Yes, sir, and more heating in the dressing-room next door,' Beth replied.

'Good, I will leave you. Call we when Mrs Haverstock is ready for me to tend her wound.'

'Mrs Thomas has taken the liberty of sending for Dr

Witherspoon, Captain. He should be here in a short while.'

Oliver frowned. He had had dealings with village sawbones before and knew that he was better qualified to dress a head injury than most country quacks. He ignored the girl's apologetic statement.

'I will wait outside; call me when you are done.' He turned at the door. 'Do not, on any account, move the bandage, is that clear?'

Beth bobbed a curtsy. 'Yes, Captain, I understand.' Satisfied, he left the ladies to their part. Outside, in the wide, carpeted passageway, all was quiet. The men had vanished, their job completed, and all signs of their muddy boots had already been removed.

He looked down at his own; they were liberally covered with grass and dirt. He shrugged; dirty boots on a clean carpet was the least of this household's problems.

The longer Mrs Haverstock remained unconscious the more concerned he became. Head injuries were the very devil. Too many times he had seen a soldier, apparently unhurt, apart from a gash on the head, sink into a coma and die. He listened to the sounds of activity from the bedchamber and wished he remembered how to pray.

Chapter Four

THE crunch of wheels on gravel alerted Mrs Thomas to Dr Witherspoon's arrival. She was opening the door as he hurried up the stairs, his black bag swinging freely from one hand.

'Thank you for coming so promptly, doctor. I will take you up to Mrs Haverstock right away.'

'The boy told me she had a head injury and was unconscious. Has there been any change?'

The housekeeper shook her head. 'No, sir. I'm afraid not.'

Oliver, who had been pacing up and down the passageway like a guard on sentry-go, also heard the visitor arrive. He halted, and leant arms folded against Sarah's closed door. If Witherspoon was half as ridiculous as his name he would not get into the room.

He glared, eyes narrowed, at the approaching figure. He relaxed a little as he appraised the tall, fair young man approaching, a friendly open smile upon his face.

The doctor extended his hand. 'Captain Mayhew, I am David Witherspoon. How is Mrs Haverstock?'

The man's firm grip and intelligent blue eyes convinced Oliver he was shaking the hand of someone who knew what he was doing.

He grinned. 'Pleased to meet you, but, forgive me for saying so, you look hardly old enough to be a medical man.'

'I passed my thirty-second birthday two months ago and I

assure you I am properly qualified. Shall we go in?'

Oliver stepped aside and the doctor tapped on the door. Hurrying footsteps crossed the room and it was opened by Beth, her eyes red.

'Come in, Dr Witherspoon, sir. My mistress has not stirred at all, not once, even when we moved her. It was like dressing a rag doll, sir.'

The young man smiled; his demeanour exuded confidence and expertise. 'I will examine her now. I am going to need your assistance but the girls can go.' With a rustle of starched aprons and blue calico the two maids vanished into the dressing-room and from there down the servants' stairs to the kitchen.

Oliver, reassured by the doctors professionalism, closed the door and followed him over to the bed. The young man spoke to Beth. 'Will you hold Mrs Haverstock whilst I take a look?'

'Yes, sir.' Beth's reply was subdued. Oliver recognized the signs and caught the girl as her knees began to buckle.

'Come along, Beth, I think we will be able to manage without you. Go and sit by the screen, out of sight, but in the room.' The girl recovered immediately she knew she was no longer required to assist the doctor in his examination and was able to walk, unaided, to the indicated position.

Oliver took her place and held Sarah gently so that she remained on her side, her injury fully visible for the first time. He was so shocked that he swore under his breath.

'God's teeth, she has been shot. That is a bullet groove. I have seen enough of them to know.'

The doctor deftly cleaned the sticky mess on the back of their patient's head, exposing a long shallow wound. It had bled profusely, as such injuries do, and required several sutures. Throughout the stitching and bandaging, Sarah had remained unconscious. When he had completed his task Dr Witherspoon finally spoke.

'I will arrange something to prevent Mrs Haverstock from

rolling onto her back, and then you can release your hold Captain.' He positioned a feather pillow to his satisfaction and stepped back. 'There, you can lie her down now.'

Oliver placed Sarah on the soft support and removed his hands. 'Will she do, doctor?'

'Yes, I believe she will. Her pulse is steady and her breathing regular. It is loss of blood, and shock, that have caused her stupor, not the injury itself.'

'How long will it be before Mrs Haverstock recovers consciousness?'

The doctor considered. He placed his hand on Sarah's face and smiled. 'She is asleep now, Captain, not unconscious. She will wake in the morning with a headache but, hopefully, nothing worse. You can question her then.'

Startled by the man's perspicacity, Oliver grinned. 'Then, I suppose I will have to contain myself until the morning.' Dr Witherspoon glanced across at the maid dozing in the chair, relieved she had not been awake to hear the captain's explanation.

'Beth?'

The girl jerked awake and rubbed her eyes. 'Yes, sir?'

'Mrs Haverstock is sleeping. You will need to sit with her tonight and send for me if she appears worse in any way. Can you do that?'

Beth smiled. 'Yes, Dr Witherspoon. I'm sorry I was no help earlier. It is blood; I can't abide it. I don't mean to, but I faint dead away – I have been like it since a child.'

'Such a reaction is not uncommon; it was not your fault. I will visit again in the morning; your mistress is in no immediate danger from her injury. We will have to wait and see if she suffers any ills from her exposure to the damp and cold.'

'It would take more than a couple of hours in the cold to overset Mrs Haverstock, sir. Many a time she's been out in a storm and returned here drenched and not even caught a sniffle from her experience.'

'Excellent! Remember, Beth, if she becomes feverish, you must send for me at once. I will be back first thing in the morning. Mrs Haverstock is to remain quiet in her bed until I have examined her.'

Outside the bedchamber door the two men exchanged worried glances.

'Come to the library, Dr Witherspoon, we need to talk.' If he thought the captain surprisingly free with his invitations the young man did not say so. In the privacy of the book-lined room Oliver firmly closed the door. 'It does not look good, Dr Witherspoon.'

'Could we dispense with formality, Captain? My given name is David.'

'And mine is Oliver. Someone tried to kill Mrs Haverstock tonight and damn near succeeded. Whoever took that shot was no amateur.'

'Why should anyone wish to harm Mrs Haverstock? She is well liked locally and takes care of her tenants as she should.'

'I was hoping you could tell me. This, I fear, is the second attempt. Mrs Haverstock and Edward disturbed intruders in the Home Wood two days ago. The boy's dog warned them and they were able to turn back and came to no harm.'

'You must inform the magistrate, Lord Hepworth, tomorrow.'

'I intend to do so. I will also send for more men; Jenkins knows the whereabouts of many of the men he served with. Most will be glad of paid employment and come at once.'

'I am not a religious man, Oliver, but one has to wonder if divine intervention did not send a military man here to act as tutor.'

'I agree that it is fortunate. No further harm will come to either my employer, or her son, whilst I am here. I can safely say that whoever it is, he is going to live to regret it.'

The doctor, looking at the formidable man, did not doubt it for a minute.

Sarah opened her eyes into a darkened room, the morning sounds hushed by drawn curtains and closed shutters. Her head hurt abominably and her limbs felt heavy. Had she caught a fever? Then, becoming fully awake, she was aware that a stiff white bandage ringed her forehead.

She ran her fingers experimentally around the circle and winced when they touched the back. The events of the previous evening came flooding back. The movement in the shrubbery, the noise, the pain, all these fell together to make an unpalatable whole. She had been shot! She tried to sit up but her head spun and she sank back. She tried again and this time managed to reach the bell to pull it.

Beth bustled in from the dressing-room. 'Mrs Haverstock, madam, you are awake. We have been so worried about you. You took a nasty tumble on your walk last night.'

Sarah did not correct her abigail's erroneous explanation. 'Beth, I need to get up. I have to talk to Captain Mayhew right away.'

'Oh no, madam, you must not. Dr Witherspoon was insistent. You have to stay in bed today. He is coming to see you after breakfast.'

'Then I will have to see the captain in here. What time is it Beth? Is he up with Edward yet?'

'It is only eight o'clock, madam. Captain Mayhew's not upstairs yet; Master Edward is still getting dressed.'

'Does Edward know of my accident?'

'No, madam.'

'Good, I will tell him myself, after I have spoken to the captain. Will you send Jack to fetch him here, please? Then help me to tidy myself. I hope I do not look half as bad as I feel.'

'Do you wish to break your fast first, madam?'

'No. I have no appetite this morning. A cup of weak tea will suffice, thank you.'

Sarah felt as though she had just completed an arduous ride when all she had achieved was a wash and change of nightwear and the donning of a pretty white lace bed-jacket. There had been nothing she could do to her hair, her head was still too sore. Now she knew the captain's role in her misfortune, she believed it was rather too late to worry about him seeing her at less than her best.

She heard him arriving outside her door and forced herself to relax. Beth would remain in the room at all times, but she was not sure how her mother-in-law, Lady Hepworth, would view her decision to entertain a man in her chamber. She smiled at the thought; Lord Hepworth would be scandalized but she was sure that she would only laugh.

Sarah was still smiling as Oliver entered. Seeing her propped on her pillows, her dark hair tumbling down her shoulders and her amazing eyes alight with laughter, caused a strange sensation to settle in his chest.

'Captain Mayhew, I am so glad to see you. I am at a loss to know how to proceed.' He stood awkwardly at the door, not sure of the correct procedure, never having been invited to visit a lady of virtue in her bedroom before. 'Please, do not hover at the door, Captain, come in. Beth is here to chaperone us . . .' She had spoken lightly, her words intended as a jest. She stopped as an awful thought came, unbidden, into her head. Did the poor man think she was trying to compromise him, trap him into marriage? Her pale complexion turned rapidly to rosy pink and her words became stuck behind her teeth. She sincerely regretted her impulsive invitation.

Sensing her distress and realizing its cause, he grinned and strolled forward nodding pleasantly to Beth, seated with her needlework at a discreet distance from the bed.

'How are you today, Mrs Haverstock? You are looking considerably improved from last night.'

'I am much recovered, thank you, Captain. And, I believe, I must also thank you for my rescue.'

He shook his head. 'No, it was Rags who found you. I find myself warming to the animal a little more each day.'

Sarah finally relaxed. 'I know exactly what you mean. Every instinct tells you he is too big, too boisterous and too loud and then he does something so remarkable you are forced to reconsider.'

He looked around and spying a plain wooden chair, picked it up one-handed and placed it at a respectful distance from the bed. Once seated he waited for Sarah to continue.

She stared at her folded hands then looked up. 'I was shot last night. Someone tried to kill me.'

He sat forward, his expression grim. 'I am afraid you are correct, ma'am. And I now believe the so-called poacher was the same person, but your dog saved you from harm.'

'But why? I have no enemies that I know of, why should anyone wish to murder me?'

'That is what I intend to find out. Do you mind answering some questions?'

'Of course not, if they will help to explain this mystery.' She paused. 'I must send word to Lord and Lady Hepworth; he is the magistrate you know.'

'It is already done; I sent Jenkins over first thing. If we are going to solve this puzzle I am going to need to know something about you and your husband.'

'I think we can eliminate my family at once. My father is a country parson, from good stock but a third son; my mother was the only daughter of the local squire. I have an older sister, who married advantageously into the peerage and now resides, comfortably, in Norfolk.'

'You are right; the threat obviously does not come from your side. So it must be linked to your husband. What can you tell me about his ancestors?'

'His grandfather married an Indian princess and became a nabob. They produced one son, Harry, who on his parents demise from cholera, returned to England and bought

Rowley Court. He married Harriet, who is now Lady Hepworth, and they had one son, Jonathan, who became my husband ten years ago.'

'How did Harry Haverstock die, might I ask?'

'He was killed in a boating tragedy on the lake. That is why we no longer have a boathouse. It was removed after the accident.'

'I see. Then your mother-in-law was left, as you were, a young widow with a small son.'

'But not for long. She was besieged by suitors, but chose to marry Lord Hepworth and they have been very happy for twenty years or more. He treated Jonathan as his own, and, although Harriet has produced only daughters, he has never once complained. The estate is not entailed so only the title goes elsewhere.'

'And you? How did you come to marry Jonathan?'

Sarah smiled sadly as she thought back. 'I was seventeen and preparing to have my London debut when Jonathan came to stay in the village: he was on a hunt for a rare orchid that was known to grow in the vicinity. I met him one Sunday, after Morning Service and that was that.' She swallowed hard and blinked, willing the unwelcome tears away. 'We had such a short time together, barely four years, before he caught a chill. This quickly turned to congestion of the lung: and he was gone. Dr Witherspoon was not here then, or perhaps he could have saved him.'

Oliver stood up and went to stare out of the window, thinking. He turned, his decision made.

'It has to be a Haverstock connection. It is possible Harry had enemies in India who have tracked down his descendants, and are only now exacting their revenge.'

Sarah shook her head, and immediately regretted it. 'Your explanation sounds highly improbable. Harry never made any attempt to disguise, or hide himself. He was well-known in London and a member of several clubs. Anyone could have found him if they had so desired.'

'It is the only theory we have, at the moment, so I suggest that you allow me to investigate it.'

'Very well. Whatever funds you need will be made available. I will send a message to my man of affairs and have him arrange it.'

'There is another point we must discuss, Mrs Haverstock. I have taken the liberty of sending for more men. Both Edward and you must be guarded at all times until whoever is behind the attacks has been apprehended.'

Sarah had not considered this. 'What will I tell Edward? I do not wish to scare him unnecessarily.'

'Tell him what happened. He is an intelligent boy, he will understand. If he knows why his liberty is to be restricted he is less likely to disobey.'

'What do you mean, restricted? Are you suggesting that we cannot go out?'

'Yes, I am. You must both stay within the formal gardens and must not venture out after sunset for any reason.'

'No riding? No visits to Hepworth House or the village?'

He shook his head. 'Absolutely not. Once my men arrive things will be a little easier; they are riflemen and will be able to protect you from further ambush.'

'I have no choice, do I? I must thank you, Captain Mayhew, for organizing this. I believe God's hand must surely have guided me in my choice of tutor.'

It was his turn to flush. He had been called many things, by women, in the past but none had ever suggested he had been God sent, but it was the second time he had heard this, so maybe there was something in it.

He cleared his throat. 'I will take my leave, now, Mrs Haverstock. Could you send word to Edward that I will not be able to commence his lessons until ten o'clock this morning?' He bowed and strode out of the open door, leaving Sarah with more questions than she had had before his visit.

'Beth, could you run up to the schoolroom and fetch Edward here to me? The sooner he knows what has transpired the better. And can you discover if Jenkins has returned from Hepworth House?'

Left on her own Sarah tried to make sense of what had happened over the past three days. Twice someone had tried to kill her and the second time they would have succeeded if she had not pulled up the hood of her cloak at the same instant the shot had been fired. The bullet must have lost some of its momentum in the heavy folds of material and so her life had been spared.

She said a silent prayer of thanksgiving; believing it must have been a guardian angel that had saved her life on both occasions.

Edward took the news with remarkable aplomb for a child of scarcely seven years. To him it was a huge adventure and he had been given a starring role. He had absolute faith in his new tutor and, Sarah sourly recognized, would be happy to remain incarcerated in the woodshed if his hero so ordained.

Dr Witherspoon duly came and went, pronouncing Sarah well enough to rise if she rested in her boudoir. She was forbidden to dress and go downstairs for another, tedious, day at least. Jenkins had returned bearing a missive that informed Sarah that she was to expect a visit that afternoon from both Lord and Lady Hepworth. His Lordship wished to speak in person to Oliver and Harriet would visit the patient in her sickroom.

Edward completed his morning studies and was released for luncheon, which, as a special treat he was to share with his mother upstairs. He was also overjoyed to discover his dog still roaming free in the house, another edict from his tutor. That Rags was now considered a suitable house pet by all was just another sign that his new mentor was a splendid fellow.

*

Lady Hepworth was shown up to Sarah's private sitting-room a little after two o'clock. She burst in, her expression anxious. 'My dear child, how dreadful, what a terrible experience!'

'It was, but I am almost fully recovered. Please come and sit down, I have so much to tell you.'

At the end of the tale Harriet frowned. 'You know, my dear, Harry once said something about Haverstock not being his real name. I believe his father fell out with his family and changed it to his mother's maiden name, not wishing to have any further contact with his past. I wonder if the problem is somehow connected to that?'

Chapter Five

'HAVERSTOCK is neither my name nor Edward's?' Sarah exclaimed. 'How extraordinary! I believe you may have found the answer to this conundrum.'

'Have I, my dear? I do not quite see how you have reached that conclusion.'

'Well, it tells us where the threat is coming from, which is a start. All we have to discover is what name Haverstock replaced and then, I am certain, we will understand.' Sarah pushed herself up, determined to find the captain and give him the information. Her head spun and she sank back defeated.

'Sit still, my dear girl, you are not well enough to be rushing about. What is it you wish to do? Can I help?'

'Could you ring the bell, I must speak to Captain Mayhew. He will be somewhere in the house with Edward.' She paused to allow the pounding in her head to subside a little. 'It appears that mathematics can be studied in a passageway, or so Edward informs me.'

'How odd! But I am sure whatever his methods Edward will learn more from him in a passageway than from you in a classroom. And the captain will be talking with Hepworth now, not with Edward.'

Sarah stiffened. 'Thank you, Harriet. It is interesting to discover you consider my skills as an educationalist as lacking as my skills as a mother.'

Harriet chuckled. 'Do not get on your high horse with me, my love. You are a wonderful mother and teacher and well you know it. But it is a well-established fact that no child learns as well from a parent as they do from another adult.'

'I apologize, I am out of sorts.' Sarah sighed. 'But it is so hard to see one's only child hanging on every word of a virtual stranger.'

'It is a great shame you and Jonathan did not produce more children. I promise you the more offspring you have the less you worry about them.'

'I would have loved to have had more babies, but we were married almost two years before Edward was born.'

'Haverstock men are not good breeders. Each of the past three generations only managed to father one child. As I now have a house full of lovely girls the fault was obviously not mine.'

'It matters little who was to blame. Without a husband I will have no further children.'

'Then remarry, my dear. You have languished alone for overlong. Jonathan would not have expected you to remain so.'

'I was over his death years ago. But I have no desire to relinquish my independence to another, even to fill my nursery. As a wealthy widow I am allowed to run my estates and manage my affairs without interference. As a wife I would no longer have that power.'

'If you met the right man, Sarah, you would feel differently. My situation was identical and I chose dear Hepworth, knowing he would not crush my spirit or curtail my interests. He has all the revenue from Harry's investments placed in my bank account to spend as I wish. And, as you know, Jonathan's inheritance came to him enhanced not diminished.'

A smart rap on the door announced Captain Mayhew's answer to his summons. 'Come in,' Sarah called, not wishing to wait for Beth to answer the door.

He entered, his face creased with concern. 'Are you worse, madam? Your summons sounded urgent.'

Sarah grinned at the tall man, liking him more each time she saw him. 'I am quite well, thank you. I do not believe you have met my mother-in-law, Lady Hepworth?'

Oliver had been unaware that Sarah had a visitor. His head snapped round and he flushed. 'I must apologize, Lady Hepworth, I did not realize Mrs Haverstock had company.'

Harriet offered her hand and he duly bowed over it. 'I will leave you now, my love, but I will come again tomorrow to see how you do. Lord Hepworth does not like to be kept waiting, Captain, so please excuse me.'

Puzzled, Sarah watched her go. Hepworth was the most obliging man alive and would happily wait all day for the woman he adored.

'Mrs Haverstock? How can I be of service?'

Flustered, Sarah glanced upwards and her eyes locked with his. A flood of warmth surged through her and this time it was not caused by embarrassment. She dragged her eyes away and studied her clenched hands. He broke the charged silence by noisily moving the vacated chair further away creating a safe space between them.

'Captain Mayhew,' Sarah stopped and laughed. 'This is ridiculous; I cannot continue to address you so formally. We are not long acquainted, but I believe we are already friends. I would like to call you Oliver and I wish you to address me as Sarah.'

'If that is your wish, then it shall be so.' He crossed his legs, his tight breeches emphasizing his muscular strength. He was not unaware of her interest and relaxed further. Things were moving on far more quickly and smoothly than he could ever have anticipated. A frightened woman with a son in danger would naturally turn to a man who could protect them.

'Oliver, I have discovered some new and vital information about my attacker.'

Instantly alert Oliver replied, 'Tell me, what have you found out?'

'Haverstock is not our original name; it appears my grand-father-in-law adopted his mother's maiden name when he travelled to India, he wished to sever all connection to his past.'

'So the attempts must originate from there? Yes, I think you could be right. However it does not explain why someone wishes you harm, and until we know your grandfather's family name we are no further forward.'

Sarah thumped her fists against the chair. 'It is so vexing! Your inquiries will be wasted if we are searching for information about Haverstocks.'

'If we investigate them we will eventually discover whom we are looking for.'

Sarah frowned. 'I do not see how?' She thought for a moment. 'Of course! We check the marriages and eventually we will find a daughter who produced a son called Richard who went to live in India.'

'You realize it will take time to find the name we want. Haverstock is not a common name, but I know of two families, apart from yours, who are so called. Each one will have to be investigated and until we have the name we seek, you and Edward will have to remain safe inside Rowley Court.'

Imprisoned in her own home? It was not a comforting notion. 'Can we not go out of doors at all?'

'No, it would be safer not to. When my riflemen arrive and are in position then it will be permissible for you to walk in the walled gardens and go out in the closed carriage.'

'I see. When do you expect these men of yours?'

He shrugged. 'Word has been sent; they should start arriving anytime from the week's end. It depends how far they have to travel.'

'Of course it does! Good heavens, Oliver, I am not a simpleton. Please do not treat me as one.'

The conversation was over. Oliver stood up, all stiff formality. 'Edward will be waiting for me, so if you will excuse me, ma'am.' He didn't wait for her reply; he spun on his heel and strode out. The door closed behind him with a decided bang.

Sarah sank back into her chair. Whatever had possessed her to speak so rudely? It had been so long since she had spoken intimately with a gentleman that maybe her social skills had deserted her. If only her head did not ache so abominably, it made it hard to organize her thoughts.

'Beth, I am feeling unwell, could you assist me to my bed.'

It was a relief to settle her head against the pillows and close her eyes. She heard Beth drawing the heavy damask curtains across the windows and the harsh sunlight was shut out. In the dimness Sarah's pain began to ease and she drifted away into a light doze. She roused enough to swallow a bowl of broth at suppertime then fell into a deep refreshing sleep.

It was the sound of horses and raised male voices that woke her early next morning. She tried moving her head from side to side before attempting to sit up. Pleased that it no longer made her feel sick and dizzy she sat up and swung her feet to the floor.

She was halfway to the door before she remembered she was in her night-rail. Exasperated she retraced her steps, grabbed her négligé and thrust her arms impatiently into the sleeves. Satisfied she was respectably covered if someone happened to glance up and saw her at the window, Sarah hurried into her private sitting-room. This had a window seat on which she could sit while she spied through the window.

Her eyes widened at the scene outside her front door. It was scarcely dawn and her drive was full of red coated, fully armed, militiamen. Lord Hepworth must have sent for them to investigate her attempted murder. Why had he done so, did he not trust Captain Mayhew and his men to find the person responsible?

A moment's doubt flickered in her mind. Was she right to put her life, and Edward's, in his hands? After all she knew only what his references had told her, and such things, as anyone could tell you, could be forged. She hadn't bothered to verify their accuracy. Now she wondered if she had been naïve not to have done so.

She retreated from the window-seat and went over to her escritoire. She would remedy that omission straightaway. Her sister's husband was well connected in the *ton*, he would know if any scandal was attached to the captain's name.

Sarah now regretted her impulsive move to allow him the use of her first name. She could not understand why she had done so; she was by nature such a cautious person. Returning to the window she watched the captain of the militia dismount and hand the reins of his huge bay horse to his lieutenant. She knew he would wish to speak with her, so she walked to the mantle and tugged the bell. Beth would be startled to receive so early a summons but she could not get dressed unaided.

Sarah went back to the window and saw the militia captain in deep conversation with the person who was ostensibly her son's tutor, but was now, quite obviously, the man in command of the operation.

She pursed her lips and her eyes glinted dangerously. Captain Oliver Mayhew was taking too much upon himself. She was the mistress here and it appeared she must, once again, clarify her position. She had quite forgotten that it was she who had given him that authority. Her memory, which up to now had always been impressive, was, like her emotions, behaving quite uncharacteristically.

Sarah flounced like a spoilt child back to her room where Beth, her cap a trifle askew, waited. 'I wish to get dressed, Beth. I will wear my rose-crêpe morning-gown and the matching slippers.' The dress was far too formal for a dawn meeting with the militia captain but it was a favourite.

The heart-shaped neckline and small sleeves emphasized her neat bust and the fashionable high waist with freely flowing skirts were, to Sarah's mind, mercifully free of frills and ruches. She believed the cut of a gown was what gave it elegance, not unnecessary adornment at hem and neck.

'I will wear a corset this morning.' If her mistress had announced she was to wash her own shift Beth could not have been more astonished, for Mrs Haverstock had not worn one since before her confinement seven years ago. 'And we must remove this hideous bandage. I cannot continue to have my hair hanging down like a hoyden.'

'I could braid it for you, madam, and hide the bandage under a pretty lace cap, that way you can leave the dressing in place.'

Sarah was about to refuse then decided that a cap might give her the air of authority she needed. 'Very well, I will wear one, but only until this can be removed.' She touched the back of the bandage with her fingertips and winced. 'Please be careful how you arrange my hair, my head is still very painful.'

'I'm not surprised, madam. You should have seen the hole the bullet made in your cloak; it was a miracle you were not killed.'

Beth stepped back and gave the dainty lace headgear a final adjustment. 'There, madam, you look a picture. I don't know why you hate them so, they suit you very well.'

Sarah risked a glance into the glass and her eyes widened. The hideous bandage had vanished under the frill of the delicate cap, which was edged with Brussels lace. Her hair, neatly braided, fell nearly to her waist.

She smiled. 'Thank you, Beth, you have worked wonders. One would not suspect I had anything other than my head underneath this.'

'And the dress looks lovely too, madam. That shade of pink has always suited you.'

Sarah hurried from the room her skirts swirling round her feet revealing a trim ankle encased in delicate pink hosiery. She could hear masculine voices in the hall. Good heavens, the wretched man had invited the militia captain inside. What next? Would he invite him to break his fast in her dining-room?

Red flags of colour stained her cheeks as she reached the head of the stairs. Both men, one of medium height and straw-blonde hair, the other tall and dark, watched a vision of loveliness descend towards them. Oliver could not tear his eyes away. How could he ever have thought this woman plain? It was only then he recognized the danger signals, the flashing eyes and tell-tale flush. What burr had she lodged under her saddle this time? He hid his smile as he waited to be told how he had offended.

Sarah paused, a corset made breathing difficult, and she feared she was going to have no air to speak. She remained on the penultimate step and hazel met grey on level terms.

'Captain Mayhew, please be so kind as to introduce me to *your* guest.' The words were honeyed but their meaning was quite clear.

Oliver coloured, amusement turned to anger in an instant. 'Forgive me, madam, this is Captain Andrews, come to search for your attackers.'

'Your servant, ma'am.' The young man bowed deeply and clicked his heels impressively like a Prussian.

'Captain Andrews,' she inclined her head an inch and waited. The two men shifted uncomfortably knowing they had breached protocol but unsure how to make amends. Sarah took pity on them. 'Did Lord Hepworth send for you, Captain Andrews? I am surprised that the attack on me warranted a full company of militia to investigate it.'

'Lord Hepworth has been concerned about several reports

of strangers in the vicinity recently, madam. He is worried that there could be insurgents gathering here and rick-burning and rioting could follow.'

Sarah opened her mouth to say that the people in her demesne were far too comfortable to riot but bit her tongue. If Hepworth had enlisted the help of this troop under false pretences then she would not be the one to point it out.

'Well, whatever the reason, I am glad you are here, Captain Andrews. You can billet your company in the barns at Home Farm; they are warm and dry and you can use the adjacent field for the horses. There is sufficient hay stored there for palliasses and fodder.'

'Thank you, Mrs Haverstock, we are here for one night only. Our presence should be enough to discourage further men from travelling to this area. We intend to search your grounds and the surrounding land today. I report to Lord Hepworth and Captain Mayhew tomorrow and then we move on.'

Her eyes narrowed. 'You will report to me before you leave, Captain Andrews, not my son's tutor.' She noticed Oliver clench his fists and instantly regretted her words.

The militia captain bowed again, but heel clicking was noticeably absent. 'I will bid you good day, Mrs Haverstock.' In the vacuum left by his departure neither spoke. Sarah too embarrassed and Oliver too angry.

They heard the soldiers remount and clatter back down the drive, the noise loud in the freezing silence of the hall. Sarah swallowed and lifted her chin defiantly. This was her house, her domain, she would not be cowed into silence by anyone.

'Captain Mayhew . . .' she faltered as he turned and raked her with a look of such bloodcurdling disdain that she felt her defiance shrivel and took an involuntary step back, raising her hand, whether to placate him or ward him off she was not sure.

'Yes, madam?' Two words but so imbued with scorn she

was unable to respond. She lowered her eyes, but could still feel the weight of his dislike boring into her. This would not do – he was her employee, not her husband. Husband? Where had that notion sprung from?

Sarah so discomfited by this ridiculous idea she inadvertently spoke what she was thinking. 'You are not my husband, sir, and have no right to stand in judgement. I am mistress here and you are in my employ.' Her hands flew to her mouth as though to push her intemperate words back where they belonged. She waited for the storm to break. To her astonishment the man, who had been glaring at her from across the hall his feet set apart and his head thrust forward, stepped back, a look of utter stupefaction on his face.

His aggressive stance relaxed and to her chagrin he threw back his head and roared with laughter. The unexpected sound ricocheted around the spacious hall and when he spluttered to a halt his brimming eyes met hers, and she felt her mouth curve reluctantly into a reciprocating smile. He extended his hand and she stepped forward and placed it in his. She looked down at their hands, hers small and pale being held gently in his calloused, battle-hardened clasp. The drumming of her heart drowned out the words that flickered in her brain. Shyly she raised her head and her limbs weakened at the intensity of his gaze. She forgot where she was and a pulsing heat surged up her arm and around her veins.

She tried to breathe deeply, to steady herself, but strangely her ribs refused to expand and her head began to swim. She pitched forward, into his waiting arms, in a dead faint.

Chapter Six

THE pungent smell of harts horn being wafted under her nose roused Sarah. She found herself lying on her bed and, thankfully, able to breathe easily once more.

Beth removed the smelling salts. 'There, there, madam, you swooned right away. It was the corset — you're not used to its restriction and could not catch your breath.'

'I am feeling well now, thank you.' Sarah glanced nervously round her chamber, half expecting the captain to be there still.

'You should have heard the Captain's language, madam, it fair made my ears burn, I can tell you.' Sarah was suddenly wide awake.

'Swearing? At you, Beth, surely not?'

Beth grinned. 'No, madam, of course not, he is a true gentleman. The abuse was directed at your corset. "An infernal contraption," was one of the more polite terms he used.'

Sarah felt the blood race from her toes to her crown, turning her scarlet with mortification. 'Beth, how could he possibly know I was wearing a corset?' Her maid belatedly realizing what her mistress was imagining now blushed rosily.

'Oh madam, you mistake my meaning. Sir felt the garment when he caught you and realized why you had fainted. He behaved exactly as he ought. He placed you on the bed and left immediately; it was I, of course, who attended to you.'

'You can consign that garment to the rubbish, Beth; I will not be wearing it again.' Then her sense of the ridiculous surfaced. 'He is quite right to call it, "an infernal contraption".' She giggled. 'The poor man has been obliged to stagger up the stairs twice, in as many days, with me in his arms.'

'Not stagger, madam, he carried you as though you were no more than thistle-down.' Beth sighed at the thought. 'He is a fine figure of a man. I've always liked a military gentleman.'

'Thank you, Beth, that will do. I cannot languish here; I have things to attend to.'

'Yes, madam.' Suitably chastened, Beth completed her duties in silence. Re-clothed in another of her morning-gowns, this one of spotted, pale-green muslin, Sarah was ready to see the man to whom she must make her apologies. What was it about him that made her behave so totally out of character?

'I will not wear a cap, please leave my hair as it is.'

In the schoolroom Edward shifted miserably on his chair, again. Exasperated Oliver reprimanded his charge. 'Edward, what is the matter? You have done nothing but fidget this past half hour.'

'I want to see my mama, she is not well, sir. Please can I go down and see her?'

Oliver's heart turned over at the piteous expression on the little boy's face. How could he have been so thoughtless? 'Of course you can, lad. I am sorry I did not suggest it myself. But she is not unwell, she merely swooned.' He hesitated then decided to tell the boy the whole. 'Do you know what a corset is, Edward?'

The boy stared at him blankly, and then nodded. 'Well, your mother had pulled hers too tight and could not breathe properly, so that is why she fainted.'

Edward grinned. 'I did not know that my mother wore such things, sir. She never has before.'

'And I doubt she will again, Edward. Now, run along and see for yourself that all is well. I will allow you thirty minutes for the visit.'

'Yes, sir, thank you, sir.' Edward's chair crashed to the floor in his eagerness and Oliver smiled ruefully. He doubted he would ever deserve such devotion from a child. Sarah was a lucky woman.

'Mama, Mama, I have come to see you.' Sarah looked up as her son erupted into the library, his face flushed from running downstairs in search of her. She stood up and opened her arms and he ran into them. She held him close and smoothed his hair, loving the silky feel underneath her fingers.

'I hope you have been given permission to be here, Edward?'

'Yes, I have half an hour to visit. Can I go out on the terrace to watch the soldiers?'

Sarah hesitated and then smiled. He could hardly be in danger with a park full of militiamen. 'Yes, darling, but stay where I can see you.' She returned to her letter. It was proving to be more difficult than she had anticipated asking her sister, Elspeth, to investigate the captain, but not allow her to suspect that she was having second thoughts about his appointment.

Satisfied, at last, the missive would achieve its object, she folded and sealed it. Jack could ride over to Hepworth House. Dear Hepworth would, as always, place his frank upon it without demure.

'It is time to come in now, Edward. You must not keep Captain Mayhew waiting.'

The boy trotted in obediently. 'Yes, Mama, I am going back up straightaway.'

'I will accompany you, love, as I wish to speak to him myself.'

The three flights of stairs made Sarah's head spin and she

was forced to grab the wooden banister for support. An arm unexpectedly encircled her shoulders.

'Allow me to assist you, Mrs Haverstock.' Oliver escorted her into the schoolroom and placed her on a convenient chair. 'You are overdoing it, Sarah; you will make yourself ill. You lost a deal of blood two days ago and it will take time for your body to recover.' His voice was gruff, his face etched with concern.

This made her task so much simpler. 'I have come to apologize for my unpardonable incivility early this morning. I am not normally so rude. I must blame my injury for my intemperate words.'

He dropped to his haunches beside her, both forgetting that Edward was hanging onto every word. He took her hands in his and held her eyes captive with the intensity of his gaze.

'It is I who must apologize, Sarah, I overstepped my authority, and will not do so again.'

Strangely unwilling to remove her hands, she smiled. 'I am sure you will not, until the next time! And I will not be rude. . . .'

'Until the next time.' He released her and straightened smoothly. A shuffle from across the room reminded them, too late, that their conversation had been overheard. For an instant their eyes locked in total understanding. 'Are you feeling well enough to return to your room, madam? Should I send for Beth to help you?'

'I am fully recovered thank you, sir. However I will take your advice and return to my room. I believe I am not as robust as I had thought.' She turned and smiled at her son. 'I will see you later, Edward, when your studies are done for the day.' Edward beamed. His delight at their growing closeness quite obvious.

The following day David Witherspoon pronounced Sarah well enough to resume her normal activities. He removed the cumbersome bandage and replaced it with a smaller dressing, reporting that the deep wound was healing well. The militia completed their search for vagrants and possible insurgents and finding nothing, departed for their next assignment. Lady Hepworth came for a second visit and Lord Hepworth accompanied his wife. Two visits in a week was an unlooked for privilege! But this time when he closeted himself with Oliver she did not resent it. Although, as she had remained in her room recuperating for the past twenty-four hours, there had been no further opportunity to fall out.

Lady Hepworth found her daughter-in-law reading in the orangery. 'My dear Sarah, I am so pleased to see you looking well. Hepworth's with your captain once again, it appears he has had some information from London he wishes to share.'

Sarah, in spite of her best resolve, felt her hackles rising. Before the arrival of Captain Mayhew, (who was *not* her captain, but Edward's,) Lord Hepworth would have shared whatever news he had with her. She frowned, the gesture pulling at her stitches unpleasantly and the sharp reminder made her smile instead.

Harriet had watched this display of emotions with interest. 'Good heavens, my love, your face is changing like a weathervane! I would dearly like to know what caused it.'

'And so you shall, Harriet. I was cross because Hepworth has not seen fit to speak directly to me, as he used to, and indeed, as he still should.' Harriet raised her eyebrows but said nothing. 'I smiled because my sour expression pulled my stitches and it was a timely reminder not to be so ungrateful.'

'He does not mean to give offence, my love; he has your best interests at heart. You have been unwell and Captain Mayhew is a military man.'

Sarah rested her hand on Harriet's plump arm. 'I know that, but it still rankles. I have been my own mistress for so long now it is hard for me to allow anyone, however well meaning, to take decisions for me.'

Harriet smiled archly. 'I do believe it is the handsome captain you resent, my dear. Now I wonder why he should stir up your passions so?'

Sarah jumped up covering her embarrassment under the pretext of ringing the bell to order her guest some refreshments. Her mother-in-law had watched her agitation with delight. Sarah had been on her own too long and her grandson's new tutor was just the man to persuade her that matrimony, with the right partner, was a positive step, not a sacrifice.

Edward joined them, released from his lessons whilst his tutor engaged with Lord Hepworth. His happy chatter filled the time, allowing Sarah to push her preoccupations temporarily to one side. But when Harriet rose to take her leave Sarah was relieved.

'I am afraid that neither Edward, nor I, can come and visit you, Harriet. Until this tiresome business is resolved it is not safe for us to venture out of doors.'

'No matter, dearest, I will come to see you both. I will bring the girls next time; they are forever asking to see their favourite nephew.'

Blessed peace fell at last on the orangery. Lord and Lady Hepworth had departed in their carriage and Edward had scampered eagerly back upstairs to resume his lessons. Sarah knew why Latin verbs and geometrical problems had suddenly become so interesting and she was not entirely happy with the thought.

Captain Mayhew, she found it difficult to think of him as Oliver, had been with them a little more than a week. How could his presence have changed both their lives so quickly? The answer to her riddle was obvious but she refused to acknowledge it, even to herself.

As usual she dined alone and afterwards returned to sit in the small drawing-room to gaze pensively into the sweet-smelling apple-wood fire. She was startled out of her reverie by a knock on the door. A maid-servant appeared.

'Captain Mayhew would like a word, madam.'

Sarah was tempted to refuse. 'Very well, show him in please.' She rose gracefully from her position by the fire, shook out her becoming dinner-gown, a dark green silk, and positioned herself in the shadows, away from the revealing lamps.

'Captain Mayhew, madam.'

Sarah's stomach lurched and she clenched her hands to stop them trembling. 'Good evening, Captain, what can I do for you?'

He halted, framed in the doorway, and Sarah thought she saw a flicker of uncertainty cross his face. Surely not? Then he closed the space between them and bowed, his blue-grey eyes giving nothing else away.

'I believe we agreed to use our given names, Sarah? I thought we were friends now?'

She kept her hands beside her and forced her lips to form a smile. 'Yes, of course we are . . . Oliver. It is hard for me; I am finding being on such terms with someone I have known for scarcely more than a week very difficult.'

He stepped away and her pulse returned to normal. 'Come and sit down, I cannot converse with you whilst you hide in the darkness.'

Reluctantly Sarah emerged from the gloom and instantly regretted it. She saw his eyes narrow and his jaw harden as he ran his gaze from head to toe, frank appreciation written on his face.

Her mouth went dry and she wanted to run away; instead she glided, apparently calm, to the *chaise-longue* and sat down. She sought a safe topic of conversation.

'Edward appears to be enjoying his lessons; I hope he is proving an able pupil?'

He cleared his throat and folded his length onto a padded, gilt-legged chair, placed opposite. 'He is an intelligent lad. I am pleased with his progress. You are welcome to come and watch us work, Sarah; your son would appreciate your interest in his studies.'

'Thank you, I would like to do that.' She finally raised her head. 'What was it you wished to see me about, Oliver?'

'I wished to pass on to you the information Lord Hepworth brought this afternoon. As far as he is aware there are no strangers, of any sort, lurking in the vicinity. The militia has, it appears, scared whoever it was, away?'

'Does that mean Edward and I are free of restrictions now?'

He shook his head. 'No, I am afraid not. I have had news that some of my riflemen will be here tomorrow and by the end of the week I should have the rest. Then I believe it will be safe for you to resume your normal routine.'

'I am anxious not to miss morning service a second time. Will we be able to leave the park to attend church this Sunday?'

'If I company you, and my men follow, then I believe it will be safe.'

Sarah's eyes widened. Had this man no idea what a small community would think if she appeared in church hanging on the arm of her son's tutor? She shuddered at the thought. 'If there is the slightest risk to either Edward, or myself, we will not go. We have a small chapel here, which will suffice for the present.' She smiled all courteous politeness. 'Was there anything else, Oliver?'

He took his cue. 'Nothing, I will take my leave. I assume you check with the housekeeper that all the doors and windows are bolted, before you retire?'

Sarah bridled. 'No, of course I do not. I have absolute faith in Mrs Thomas's efficiency in such matters.'

'I see. If that is the case, I will check them myself before I leave. No doubt your housekeeper can bolt the front door securely after me.'

He left Sarah no time to reply. She was left staring at the

closed door, fuming at his impertinence.

When Sarah settled down for the night she was glad she could sleep easily knowing her home was safe. She heard Rags patrolling the corridors outside; did he seem a little more restless this evening? Then she heard her door softly open and sat up. A sliver of light appeared and a small white shape stepped into her room.

'Can I come in with you, for a bit, Mama? I keep hearing noises and I cannot sleep.'

Sarah threw back the comforter and welcomed her son into her bed. 'Come in, darling, you are shivering. I expect you had a nightmare. Rags is outside and would soon let us know if anything was wrong, would he not?'

Edward, half asleep, mumbled his agreement and snuggled down into the soft embrace of his mother's arms. Lovingly, Sarah stroked his head and kissed his sleeping eyes. She sighed sadly, knowing that such nocturnal visits would not continue for much longer. But she would let him sleep for a little while, before returning him to his own bed in the nursery. Content, she pulled the covers up and lay back on the pillows, feeling the rhythmic breathing of her son against her shoulder.

She drifted into a deep, refreshing slumber and dreamt of the time when Edward was a baby and sat on his doting father's knee. Only the father was not Jonathan, it was a grey eyed man, with a devastating smile.

It was pitch black and there was no moon to spill its silvery light on the walls of Rowley Court. If it had, one of the watchers might have spotted a dark shape climbing up the ivy-covered wall beneath Edward's bedchamber. The intruder balanced skilfully and slipped a stiletto between the window frames and silently moved the latch across. The window slipped upwards and he slithered in. Minutes later he reappeared and scrambled down the wall and vanished into the darkness.

Rags's frantic barking dragged Sarah awake. The dog was throwing himself against the door in his effort to gain entry. She scrambled out of bed and hastily lit her bedside candle. There had to be something wrong for the dog to be making so much noise outside her chamber.

Chapter Seven

SARAH flung open the door but Rags, surprisingly, did not rush in as she had expected.

'What is it boy? Why are you making so much noise?'

The sound of someone banging furiously at the front door and shouting demands to be let in, gave her no time to think. She ran back into her room and hastily donned her robe before rushing downstairs to unbolt the door.

Two of Captain Mayhew's men, Jenkins and Peters, were waiting outside.

'Good evening, ma'am. Is anything amiss? We heard the dog barking and have come to investigate.'

'As far as I can see everything is as it should be.' She stepped aside. 'Please come in and look around. Is the captain here?'

Jenkins shook his head. 'No, madam, but he has been sent for and will be here in a moment.'

Sarah followed the men back upstairs where the dog was still barking and growling ferociously. It was only then she became aware of a strange smell. She sniffed then froze.

'Jenkins, I can smell smoke.'

'Yes, ma'am, so can I. Something is on fire.' He gave the man beside him a sharp push. 'Go back down and bang the gong, Peters. We have to get everyone out of here.'

Sarah did not wait to be told. She fled up the stairs and back into her chamber. 'Wake up, Edward, quickly, we must get out of the house, there is a fire somewhere upstairs.' She shook him again more urgently and finally he stirred and allowed himself to be bundled out of bed and enveloped in a knitted shawl. It was Rags's cold nose in his hand that brought him to full consciousness.

'Rags is here, Mama? Is something wrong?'

'Yes, dear, there is a fire upstairs, we have to go outside until it is safe.' Edward needed no further urging. He had once watched a cottage burn and remembered the speed with which the flames took hold. Hand in hand they ran down the stairs, the dog bounding beside them. They met Oliver racing in. He saw his charge, safe beside his mother, and halted.

'Thank God, Edward, you are safe.'

Edward grinned. 'I was with Mama, sir, not in my room. And Rags woke us up. Is he not a clever dog?'

'He is, lad. Now, outside, both of you. We have to rouse the rest of the house and get them out before we can tackle the blaze.'

Several of the house staff already milled in the central area in front of the marble steps. Sarah handed Edward into the care of his nursemaid Sally, and walked briskly over to Mrs Thomas. 'You are here quickly, Mrs Thomas. I am glad to see you. Are all the girls out yet?'

'Yes, madam. We heard the dog barking and were already awake. Sally smelt the smoke, it was coming from Master Edward's room. Luckily she knew he had gone downstairs to you, she heard him go.'

'So no one is missing. Can you check please, Mrs Thomas?' The housekeeper called the frightened group to her side and did a quick headcount.

'Yes, madam, they are all here, safe and well. We owe our lives to the dog, that's for certain.'

'I must go and tell Captain Mayhew that everyone is out. Then he can try and put out the fire. God willing, he is not too late.'

'Rags is a hero, Mrs Thomas. He has saved everyone tonight, has he not?'

'Indeed he has, Master Edward. Now, here comes madam, with news.'

Sarah shivered as she stumbled back, in the dark, to join her son. The night was chill and none of them were dressed. The men had vanished into the house carrying buckets snatched from the stables. It was a long climb from the pump in the kitchen to the top floor. She prayed Oliver would have enough men to complete the chain.

She turned to the huddle of women. 'Come, let us go to the stables. We can shelter there; at least it will be warmer than waiting outside. And as all the men are helping inside the house we will have the place to ourselves.' She led the way around the drive, through the arched carriageway and into the cobbled stableyard. The loose boxes were closed but she could hear the horses moving restlessly, disturbed by the unusual activity. She was relieved to see that some lamps had been lit and hung, flickering, against the walls, making pools of welcome light.

Edward ran ahead and unbolted the tack room. 'It is snug in here, Mama. I often come in to talk to Jack. And there are stools and boxes we can sit on.'

'Well done, Edward. Come along everyone. It will be a trifle crowded but at least we will be warm.' Sarah removed a convenient lantern from a hook and took it in with her.

The subdued and shivering group of women followed her into the small room, glad to be out of the cold. May evenings, as Sarah had discovered a few evenings ago, could be deceptively cold. She placed the lantern onto a peg and then kindled two more from its flames. Edward was enjoying the adventure and, as the only male in evidence, decided it was his place to take charge.

'Mama, you must sit on this stool, Mrs Thomas, you take this one.' Half smiling, Sarah allowed herself to be guided to the seat indicated and, trying hard to ignore the dirt and cobwebs, gathered in the folds of her nightwear and sat down.

Mrs Thomas followed; the rest of the party perched and leant wherever there was a space available. Edward regarded them with satisfaction. 'Shall I close the door to keep out the cold?'

Sarah shuddered. 'No, leave it, my dear; we will be quite warm enough with it open.' She smiled to herself. It would be ironic if, having escaped from the fire, they all perished from suffocation.

Mrs Thomas spoke what they were all thinking. 'How did a fire start in Master Edward's room, madam? Sally swears she did not leave a candle burning.'

Sarah believed she knew, but decided such knowledge was best kept to herself. 'No one is blaming Sally, Mrs Thomas. We must pray that Captain Mayhew, and the men will be able to put it out before too much damage has been done.'

Edward, from his vantage point of the door, pronounced loudly, 'If the fire was bad, Mama,we would be able to see it and hear it, and I can hear nothing and there is no red glow in the sky is there?'

Sarah got up, with difficulty, and went to join her son. She tilted her head to listen. 'No, you are quite right, Edward. There is no sound of burning.' She knew he was remembering the ravenous flames that had devoured the farm cottage the previous autumn. 'It is a good sign. I am sure they will put out the fire and we will all be back indoors in no time.'

'I did not light a candle to come down, Mama,' Edward said in a small voice.

'I know you did not, love, for I thought you were a ghost drifting into my room.'

He giggled, as she had intended. 'Did I scare you, Mama? If I had known I would have groaned as well.'

'It is as well you refrained, my dear, or it would have been my screams of terror that roused the house, not your dog barking.'

'You are a young rascal, Master Edward,' the housekeeper said, chuckling. 'Fancy trying to scare your poor Mama!'

'I was funning, Mrs Thomas. I would never do anything to hurt her.'

'Why, Master Edward, I know that. We all know no lady could have a better son.' She shuffled her ample frame uncomfortably on the stool. 'Can you hear anything at all out there, Master Edward? Shouting and such like?'

Edward stepped out, trailing his blanket in the mire. 'No, Mrs Thomas, I can hear nothing. Can I go and see what is happening, Mama?'

'No, Edward, you cannot. And pick up your blanket, it is getting dirty.' The little boy hastily pulled the cover back round his shoulders and returned to stand beside his mother. Rags pressed his warm weight against his legs and licked his hand. Absently Edward scratched the dog's head and the animal sighed happily.

Now their fear had dissipated and they were warm, the women relaxed and conversation flowed. Beth came to stand beside her mistress. 'Do you think we will be out here long, madam?'

'I have no idea, Beth. Even if they do douse the fire quickly the upper floor will be unusable. Smoke gets everywhere even when the flames have not.'

'Master Edward can move downstairs and he can take his lessons in the library, but where will we sleep, madam?'

Sarah closed her eyes, her head hurt and she was finding it hard to concentrate. 'I have not considered, Beth. Mrs Thomas will have to organize things. Why not ask her?'

Beth moved away and in the background Sarah heard the women discussing how they would be accommodated if their sleeping quarters had been ruined. She leant heavily against the door-frame, wishing she was back in the comfort of her bed.

'Mama, Mama, I can hear someone coming.' Sarah jerked back to full consciousness; she too heard heavy footsteps crunching towards the stables. She straightened and gathered her robe tighter.

'Captain Mayhew?' She stared, not certain the smoke-grimed man now approaching was, indeed, Oliver.

There was a flash of white in the blackened face. 'Mrs Haverstock, I am pleased to tell you the blaze is out. It had not had time to take hold and it is only one room that is severely damaged and that is not beyond repair.'

Sarah stepped forward, holding her hands out in greeting. 'Thank you, Captain. I am so grateful to you and the men. Rowley Court, itself, could have been lost tonight.'

He quietly pressed her fingers and released them, leaving black smudges behind. 'You can return to your rooms now, madam.'

'And the others? How badly smoke-damaged are their rooms?'

'Not at all. The smoke reached only the school-rooms and the nursery and they will only require a thorough clean to be habitable again.'

'Mrs Thomas, did you hear that?' Sarah turned to her housekeeper. 'You can all go back now. I do not expect anyone to rise early today. You must all sleep in.'

Beaming, Mrs Thomas came forward. 'Thank you, madam. Come along girls, it is safe to return now, thanks to the men.'

Sarah stood aside, holding Edward's hand, and allowed them to troop past, trailing shawls and comforters, some with bare feet and others in clogs, all eager to reclaim the warmth and comfort of their beds. They disappeared, chatting, into the night leaving the stables strangely silent behind them. Edward tugged her hand. 'Mama, I am cold now, can we go back up, please?'

Ashamed that she had remained, mesmerized by the man standing quietly in front of her, Sarah squeezed her son's hand reassuringly. 'Yes, love, let us go. Thank you, once again, Oliver. We will talk tomorrow about this?'

He reached out and brushed a cobweb gently from her cheek. 'Yes, Sarah, we will. Now, go, you are both shivering. It is too cold to stand here talking.' They heard the sound of laughing and rough voices heading their way. The stable hands were returning.

'Goodnight, Oliver.' Sarah, still clutching Edward's hand, turned and fled back to the house forcing the men to jump aside as she ran past.

When Sarah finally roused it was almost ten o'clock. Even with the windows open the room smelled of damp material and stale smoke. She slipped out of bed, leaving Edward still sleeping peacefully, his small form barely discernible under the feather comforter.

She drew the hangings quickly around the bed and rang the bell. Beth appeared immediately. 'Beth, have you been upstairs to inspect the damage? Does Edward have any clothes left to wear?'

'Yes, madam. It is only his bedroom that is severely burnt. His dressing-room escaped the flames. Sally is sorting out his garments: they need airing because they smell of smoke but apart from that they were undamaged.'

'Excellent. Have Sally attend him here. Let him sleep until then.' Sarah hardly noticed what she was dressed in, she wished to go upstairs and review the room for herself. 'Is the captain here, Beth, do you know?'

'Yes, madam. He is in the study with Lord Hepworth.'

'Lord Hepworth? When did he arrive?' Her tone was clipped, her eyes flashed dangerously.

'Hurry up, Beth. I must go down at once.'

Beth tied the bow of the becoming pale green sash that encircled the high waist of Sarah's leaf-green, muslin gown. 'There, madam, I have done. You look lovely if you don't mind me saying so.'

'Thank you, Beth. Please stay here until Sally arrives to look after Edward.' Sarah stalked out, her cheeks bearing tell-tale patches of colour. Outside the study door she paused and took a moment to calm herself. It was not Hepworth's fault that the wretched captain had overstepped his boundaries yet again and she had no wish to offend him.

The murmur of male voices was clearly audible even through the thickness of the door. She hesitated, should she knock? Of course not! It was her study the men were in. She opened the door and stepped inside. Two heads turned as one. Pale blue eyes widened in surprise, dark grey narrowed with amusement.

'Ah . . . Sarah, come in. You will see that I asked Lord Hepworth to attend us.'

Sarah almost snorted and scarcely refrained from stamping her foot. 'Why did you not wait until *we* had spoken?'

'The matter was urgent and I did not wish to wake you, Sarah. Would you not have sent for Lord Hepworth?'

Sarah's breath hissed through her clenched teeth. 'Of course I would. How many times do I have to say this? I make the decisions here, no one else.'

The words hung icily in the silence. Hepworth shuffled the papers spread out in front of him on the table and waited for the explosion.

'Please excuse us for a moment, Lord Hepworth.' Oliver took Sarah's arm and guided her back into the corridor before she could protest. She opened her mouth but he shook his head. 'No, Sarah, not here. In the library, where we can be private.' Still holding her arm he bundled her unceremoniously through the door and closed it firmly behind him. Then he released her and leant back, arms folded, eyes glinting, against the door, blocking her escape. 'Now, my dear, let me have it with both barrels. I have overstepped the mark, again, and am prepared to take my punishment.'

Sarah almost gobbled with anger and frustration. 'How dare you laugh at me Oliver Mayhew? Is it not enough that you make free with my home and servants?' He smiled down at her and braced himself for a physical attack. 'You are impossible! If Edward did not love you I would dismiss you now, this instant.'

'And you, my dear, are totally captivating when you are angry.' Before she realized his intention he stepped forward and holding her face still, kissed her, hard, on her opened lips.

Sarah's hands flew to the offended area and she took an involuntary step backwards, her eyes round with shock. The roar of laughter that bounced around the room so surprised her that she found herself smiling in response.

Eyes brimming they regarded each other, knowing their relationship had changed irrevocably, but not sure quite how to deal with it. Still smiling, Sarah shook her head. 'You should not have done that, Oliver. It was unfair.'

'I know it was, and I most humbly apologize.' She did not notice that he omitted to add that he would never repeat the offence. 'Shall we return to the study, Sarah? Lord Hepworth will be waiting.'

'Yes, of course.'

All desire to laugh abruptly left her as she walked slowly back to rejoin her guest. She got straight to the point. 'Hepworth, last night someone tried to burn down this house.'

'Yes, my dear, I know.' He frowned and nodded gravely. 'I am afraid it is worse than that.'

'Worse?' Sarah echoed, feeling sick.

'Yes, we believe the intruder did not climb into Edward's room by chance. He set the fire there deliberately.'

Sarah was glad she had not broken her fast as a wave of nausea made her gag. 'If Edward had not been with me ...' Her voice trailed away as she watched the two men, grim faced, nod. It was too awful to contemplate; her beloved son

75

had nearly met his death in the most horrible way imaginable. Without a sound she sank into a dead faint and Oliver leapt forward to catch her.

Chapter Eight

'MRS Haverstock? How are you feeling now?' The questioner's voice appeared familiar but it was not Oliver speaking. Sarah's eyes blinked open and she saw Dr Witherspoon standing by her bed. She tried to sit up but her head spun unpleasantly. 'No, lie still. There have been too many unpleasant shocks in too short a time. I should not have allowed you to get up so soon, Mrs Haverstock. I will not make the same mistake again.'

'I do not remember how I got here. What happened? Have I been unconscious for long, doctor?'

He shrugged. 'Long enough for me to be called: an hour or so, no more.'

Events were beginning to come back. The awful realization that someone unknown had tried to murder her son, and then the numbing darkness claiming her. 'Oh dear! Poor Captain Mayhew, he has now carried me upstairs three times in as many days.'

The young man smiled. 'Exactly! This time, Mrs Haverstock, I must insist you remain in your bed until you are fully recovered.'

'How long will that be?'

'Several days, possibly a week. You need absolute rest – no excitement – no worries. You must leave the running of the household to your capable housekeeper and your son's welfare to Captain Mayhew.'

Sarah felt too weak to argue. 'I would like to see Captain Mayhew, please. Could you send Beth to fetch him?'

Dr Witherspoon removed himself to the window to await Oliver's arrival. He stared, a slight frown upon his brow, at his patient. With her complexion so pale and her frequent swoons, he was worried that the injury to her head was more serious than he had first thought. There was a soft tap on the door.

Sarah smiled weakly. 'Come in, Oliver, we need to talk.' Her voice was quiet but the tone firm.

Oliver raised an eyebrow towards the window and Dr Witherspoon took the hint. 'I will wait downstairs, Mrs Haverstock. Please do not tire my patient, Captain Mayhew. She needs no further excitement.'

Oliver gestured impatiently with one hand but did not answer. His face was almost as pale as hers. He came forward, a tentative smile on his face. They didn't hear the click as the door shut and they were left alone.

'Sarah, my dear, I am so sorry to see you unwell again.'

'It is I who must apologize. Until recently I have never fainted in my life. You must think me a feeble sort of woman.'

He drew up a chair and placed it close beside the bed. He reached out and took her cold hand. 'You? Feeble? Never! You are the strongest woman I have ever met. You received a serious head wound a few days ago and rose from your sickbed too soon, that is all.'

Sarah had not the energy to remove her hand. Indeed the transfer of warmth was rather pleasant. She tried to gather her wits; there were important issues to discuss, but Oliver was sitting so close she found it hard to think.

To her relief he released her and moved his chair away and she found she was able to breathe again without restriction. What she had to say could only be said in private.

'Beth, leave us please.' The girl obediently departed but her face showed her disapproval. 'Oliver, it appears I must stay an invalid for some days.' She paused. He nodded. 'It is obvious that both my life and Edward's are at risk.' She stopped again and closed her eyes, marshalling her thoughts. What she was going to ask the man watching her so closely was going to be difficult.

'I will take care of you and Edward, Sarah, if you will give me leave.'

Her eyes flickered open and she smiled again, relieved that he had given her the opening she needed. 'Thank you, Oliver. I wish you to take over the management of the estate as well but I fear Lord Hepworth would expect to be given that role. He will not be happy that I have entrusted such authority to Edward's tutor.' She had his full attention. Did he suspect what she was going to suggest?

'If you were my affianced husband there would be no problem.'

Oliver leant forward, his expression gave nothing away. 'You are suggesting a temporary arrangement? An engagement with no substance?'

She nodded. Surely he had not thought she meant anything else? 'I also wish you to live here, at Rowley Court. I will feel safer with you under the same roof. Only as my fiancé could this be considered acceptable.'

Oliver didn't hesitate. 'I think it is an excellent plan, and I am quite prepared to enter in to such an arrangement if it will make you and Edward safer. Do you wish me to send a notice to *The Times*?'

'Yes, please do that. You realize that neither Lord nor Lady Hepworth must suspect the truth? Our liaison must appear genuine.' Her voice faltered. She could feel her strength ebbing. 'I wish you to be Edward's guardian should I not recover. Is that clear?'

Oliver left his chair to kneel beside her bed. He took both her hands and squeezed them hard, jerking her awake. 'What fustian you speak, my dear girl! You will be up and about in a few days; you are not on your deathbed.' The fierce certainty in his voice reassured her. 'This contract between us need remain only until we have solved the mystery surrounding the attacks. Do you agree to this?'

'I do. Thank you for your understanding, Oliver. I think it would be better if Edward believes this is a genuine arrangement too. We must tell him together, before we tell anyone else.'

He turned and tugged the bell. Beth appeared, her expression guarded. 'Yes, madam?'

'Please fetch Edward. He will be in the library with Sally.'

Oliver stared after her, his eyes narrowed with displeasure. 'That girl is insolent, Sarah.'

'Hush, she has been my abigail since my marriage and has only my best interests at heart. Naturally she disapproves of us being closeted, unchaperoned, in my bedchamber. When she knows we are betrothed she will be all smiles.'

He relaxed and grinned. 'I do not suppose Lord Hepworth, or Dr Witherspoon, are overjoyed about this meeting, either.'

The sound of running childish footsteps approaching down the corridor caused Oliver to scramble to his feet. He removed the chair and stood back, at a suitable distance from the bed, his back to the window.

Edward burst in. 'Mama, I did not know you had been taken ill.' He ran across and flung himself, tearfully, onto the bed.

'I am just a little weak, my dear, nothing worse. Dr Witherspoon thinks I got up too soon after my accident. There is nothing serious for you to worry about.'

The small, tousled-haired boy rubbed his eyes dry with his fists. It was only then he became aware that his tutor was standing, watchful, by the window. He glanced across and risked a small smile of greeting. It was returned full measure.

Sarah took her son's grubby hand. 'Edward, Oliver and I have something wonderful to tell you.'

'I know! I know!' Edward screeched, his face split by the widest smile. 'You are to be married? I am right, am I not?'

She felt a moment's guilt at his delight. Was it right to deceive him, when he so obviously desired this match? Oliver stepped forward and Edward flew into his embrace.

'Can I call you Papa? Must I still call you sir?'

Oliver laughed and held the boy close, his eyes met Sarah's and she shrugged helplessly, then nodded her agreement. 'It is a little premature, my boy, but as your mother is agreeable, you have my permission to address me so, if that is what you wish.' He lowered the child to his feet and ruffled his hair affectionately. 'You do realize, Edward, what else calling me Papa means?'

Edward shook his head, unsure. 'No, tell me.'

'I am no longer solely your tutor, but have control of all your life. If you are disobedient I have the right to beat you!' He scowled ferociously and Edward giggled.

'I am never disobedient, am I, Mama? Will you teach me how to shoot and play billiards now?'

'If I must, young man. Now kiss your mother and run along. Your grandpapa is in the library, he will be pleased to see you, but you may not tell him our good news. I must do that.'

Edward held Sarah's hand and whispered, 'I am so pleased. I prayed that he would become my papa. He will take care of us now, we will both be safe.'

'We will, darling, we will. Now, do as you were bid, and go down to the library. You may come and see me later.'

Oliver stepped up to the bed, bent down and dropped a feather-light kiss on Sarah's mouth. 'I will leave you now, my love; I must speak to Lord Hepworth before Edward forgets his promise and gives away our secret.' He winked as he straightened, well aware he was taking the pretence further than she wished.

Beth hurried forward as the door closed behind him. 'Oh,

81

madam, I'm so pleased. We can all rest easier in our beds if the captain is in charge of everything.'

Sarah settled back, pleased her subterfuge had been so well received. Belatedly she realized she had not discussed the extra remuneration due to Oliver. When she saw him next she would assure him he would be well paid for his services. Masquerading as her fiancé was no more than an extension of his employment after all.

Lord Hepworth greeted the announcement with unrestrained delight. 'Well done, my boy, well done! My dear wife will be overjoyed as she has been hoping young Sarah would take the plunge again.'

'Thank you, my lord. It is a relief that you are pleased with our news. We have not known each other long and we feared we might be accused of being too hasty.'

'Not a bit of it, my boy. I knew the instant I set eyes on my Harriet, and she on me. The sooner you are wed the better, if you do not mind my saying so. Sarah and Edward need your protection. There is some devil out to harm them and until we have him stopped their lives are at risk.'

'That is why we decided to announce it now. I need to be on hand at all times to keep them both safe.'

'Ah! I understand, as an unattached gentleman it would have been impossible for you to move into Rowley Court. Good God! The village tabbies would have made your ears burn.'

Oliver grinned wryly. He thought the engagement of a penniless, ex-army officer to a wealthy widow would cause almost as much gossip. 'The last four of my riflemen will be here tomorrow, or the next day. I will then have ten trained and fully armed men to patrol the grounds. That will be more than enough to keep them from harm.'

'Excellent, excellent! I see you have it all in hand, my boy. I will arrange for a basket of dainties to be sent over for Sarah.

There are pineapples and peaches ready in my hothouse.' He nodded towards the eagerly listening Edward. 'I shall have Cook put in some gingerbread for you as well.'

Lord Hepworth rose to his feet and offered his hand to Oliver. His grip was surprisingly firm for a man of his advancing years. 'I will bid you good day, my boy. I expect Harriet and the girls will be pestering to come over and talk weddings.' At the captain's look of horror he laughed. 'Never fear, I can put them off for a day or two. Give Sarah time to recover.'

'Thank you, sir, that would be appreciated. Sarah has undergone too much excitement and stress in the last few days. She needs to recoup and recover.'

'I will see myself out. I do not stand on ceremony here, you know.'

Oliver bowed and watched the stocky, grey-haired figure depart; a slight frown marred his features. Events were moving on too swiftly and decisions were being taken out of his hands. He had chosen to accept the post as tutor to Edward Haverstock after having seen Sarah for himself. It had always been his intention to marry her but on *his* terms. Somehow she had pre-empted him with this fallacious engagement, forced him into a situation he was no longer in control of.

He had wanted Sarah to fall in love with him, to be so besotted she would deny him nothing. That his affections should become engaged instead had not been part of his scheme. He felt vulnerable and at a loss to know how to proceed.

Angrily, he slammed his fist on the desk, the pain clearing his mind and helping him to focus his attention on the main matter, that of unmasking the villain who was attempting to murder his fiancé and her son.

Upstairs Sarah somehow slept through the banging and clattering that accompanied the clearing of Edward's bedchamber. Jack and Billy, an under-gardener, had been given the unenviable task of removing the incinerated bed and charred remains of curtain, commode and carpet.

The two youngsters had removed the damaged window-frame and were throwing the debris out of the window where it fell three floors to land, noisily, on the terrace below. That they had thought to spread a layer of straw to protect the slabs from damage was an admirable notion. Unfortunately their mathematics was sadly askew and most of the jettison from the room was missing the straw altogether.

Edward, hearing the delightful sound of falling carpentry, raced upstairs to join in the fun. It was there Oliver discovered him, so soot-covered he resembled a blackamore and was only distinguishable from his fellow dismantlers by his size.

'Enough! Stop this at once!' Oliver roared over the banging. Instant silence fell and three grimy faces turned to look, their teeth white slashes as they gaped at the furious giant towering over them. It was Edward who found the courage to speak.

'Should we not be doing this, Papa? Are we doing something you dislike?' His ingenuous enquiry halted Oliver, his angry words remained unspoken. He looked round the blackened ruin of the room, already half cleared.

He shook his head in bafflement, being with Edward was making him turn soft. His next words held no trace of annoyance. 'No, lad, I came up merely to suggest to you all that it might be a good idea to look out of the window.'

Puzzled, the older boys rushed to the empty frame, Jack instinctively putting his arm across the gap to prevent Edward coming too close. They surveyed the chaos they had caused below. They saw an almost pristine layer of glowing yellow straw below, surrounded on all sides by shards of charred wood, mattress, and burnt carpet pieces.

Jack stepped back and drew Edward away from the window with him.

'We had no idea, Captain, sir. We thought all this,' he gestured vaguely round the ruined room, 'was landing safely on the straw we put down. I don't understand how it is all over the lawn, the terrace and the flowerbeds.' His voice held genuine bewilderment, as if some malign fate had spread the debris deliberately in every place apart from the one it was intended to be in.

Oliver stared from one miscreant to the other and reluctantly his mouth began to curl. These boys were working so enthusiastically and were genuinely mystified about the inappropriate whereabouts of their labours.

'Are you dropping your rubbish or throwing it out?' He was trying hard to disguise his mirth.

Jack looked from Billy to Edward and then said happily, 'Throwing it – that way Edward does not need to go near the window, sir.'

Oliver swallowed. 'Exactly, Jack. The straw is directly underneath the window, ideal if you were dropping it but not for hurling it through the window as you appear to be doing.'

Edward came over and shyly touched his future father's hand. 'Are we in trouble, Papa? Are you very angry?'

Oliver's heart turned over. He held the boy to him and said gruffly. 'No, Edward. It was a genuine mistake. No real harm has been done, yet.' Jack and Billy understood the message.

'We will go down and clear everything up before we do any more, sir. We need to move the straw as well.'

'I think it would be better if you desisted from throwing anything out of here. Make a pile over here. I will get someone else to remove it.'

'Yes, sir. Sorry, Captain.' Jack's reply was subdued. Men had been turned off for lesser offences, they were lucky to have got off without even a serious reprimand.

Oliver nodded pleasantly and escorted his small charge

from the room. 'Come, lad, I will take you down to Sally. She must organize a bath and change of clothes before you go to visit your mama.' Edward allowed himself to be led downstairs quite unaware of the maelstrom of unexpected emotions he had released in Oliver's head.

Chapter Nine

THREE days after Sarah had been confined to her bed, Dr Witherspoon declared her sufficiently recovered to spend the day reclining in her boudoir.

The announcement of her engagement had appeared in *The Times* that morning. Seeing it in print, and knowing all her friends and family would see it as well, made her wonder if she had made the right decision. She folded the paper and handed it back to Oliver.

'I hope my father and sister received my letter before they read this.'

'Does it matter? You are no longer a debutante who needs your family's permission before making your decisions.'

'I know that, but strangely enough they care for my welfare and would be concerned if they thought I had become engaged to someone unsuitable.'

His smile did not reach his eyes. 'Like me? Will they consider me an unscrupulous fortune hunter?'

'Please do not be ridiculous, Oliver. Of course, I am not referring to you. But they have not met you and do not know you as I do.'

'But we do not really know each other do we, Sarah? We have been acquainted scarcely a month, after all.'

'A week was long enough to know you are a brave and resourceful man with a natural affinity with children.' She grinned at him. 'It was also long enough for me to know you can be arrogant, opinionated and short-tempered.'

'And I knew instantly that you are a lovely, intelligent, independent young woman with a sharp tongue and high opinion of herself.'

They stared at each other for a moment, neither sure whether to be flattered by the compliments or offended by the criticism.

Sarah broke the silence. 'Well, we have seen both the worst and the best and we are still friends, are we not?'

'More than friends, I hope, my dear.' Oliver was suddenly beside her and her pulse accelerated. His dark features were so close she could see the faint white line of an old battle scar that ran from the corner of his left eyebrow back across his forehead. Her fingers itched to trace its path and bury themselves in the thickness of his hair. She should stop this; one word would send him away. He would never take what was not freely offered.

It was so long since she had felt the comfort of a man's arms around her that she raised her eyes and gave him the permission he required. He slid his arms around her and, pulling her gently forward, lowered his mouth to cover hers in a kiss of such devastating sweetness that her lips parted, allowing him to explore as he wished.

Her hands linked round his neck, holding him captive, reluctant to end the embrace. Finally he raised his head, his eyes dark with desire, his cheeks flushed. He gazed down at the woman in his arms, her eyes soft and loving, her mouth swollen from his kisses, and knew that if he did not pull back, he would not be able to stop.

Slowly he removed his arms. 'We must stop now, Sarah, or this will reach a place where it becomes impossible to turn back.'

Sarah moved her head restlessly, her hands dropped back and her eyes fluttered shut, then opened. Her cheeks were pink, not with desire but with embarrassment. How could she have behaved so wantonly? This man was not her real fiancé; he was her employee and had no right to take such liberties with her person.

'This will not do, Oliver. It must not happen again, do you understand? You have taken shameful advantage of me when I am too weak to refuse.'

He leapt angrily to his feet. His desire to make love to Sarah instantly turned to an urgent wish to ring her neck. 'Good God, Sarah, I did not ravish you! It was you holding me captive, not the other way round.'

The fact that this statement was patently true only inflamed her ire. 'How dare you suggest such a thing? You forget yourself, Captain Mayhew. You are being employed to take part in a masquerade. This does not give you leave to act as if the arrangement is genuine.'

'Thank you for making my position clear, Mrs Haverstock. I must apologize for my presumption. In future at meetings I will be strictly professional. Do I have your permission to leave?' His icy sarcasm and glare of total disgust made Sarah regret her intemperate words. Too late to recall them now, the damage was done, their friendship ruined.

Gathering the remnants of her pride she schooled her face to reflect none of her inner anguish. 'Yes, that will be all, Captain. I am sure you have pressing duties elsewhere which will occupy all your time in the future.'

He nodded curtly and without bothering to answer, strode from the room. Sarah swallowed a sob, not sure how she could have turned something so pleasurable into such an unmitigated disaster. She closed her eyes and felt hot tears pricking behind her eyes. What was the matter with her? She had swooned and wept more often in the past weeks than in the last five years. It really would not do; she was made of sterner stuff than this. She must not let the fact that someone was trying to murder Edward and herself cause her to behave in such a feeble way.

She scarcely had time to recover her equilibrium before her maid tapped on the open door. 'Lord Hepworth has sent a box over for you, madam. Should I have it brought up?'

'No, thank you, Beth. Have it sent to the kitchen; Cook will know how to deal with it. I am not feeling too well, could you assist me to my bed?'

Even with her maid's strong arm the journey to her bed seemed overlong. Finally the curtains rattled shut and left her in the welcome sun-dappled dimness to contemplate her future. She realized she was playing a dangerous game. Oliver was not a man like Jonathan whom she could bend to her will. He was hot-blooded and was able to inflame her passions in a way her husband never had. She closed her eyes and let her mind drift hack to the few moments she had spent in his arms. Just the thought made her feel restless and her skin flecked with unwelcome heat.

It would not do! She was a respectable widow, not a member of the *demi-monde*. Such feelings could only be considered acceptable for a married woman. Slowly, languorously, she stretched, the coolness of the cotton sheets welcome on her overheated limbs.

As she drifted off to sleep she smiled, maybe the engagement should become genuine? Being married to someone like Oliver would definitely have many advantages.

'Here you are, Master Edward, Lady Hepworth has sent you some gingerbread men.' Mrs Thomas held out a sweet-smelling ginger confection in the shape of a little person. Edward took it eagerly. He sniffed it appreciatively, then his nose curled and he held it at arm's length.

'This smells strange, Mrs Thomas, not the way it usually does.' He wafted it under the cook's nose.

'Hold still, Master, let me have a sniff. Yes, you're right, maybe this one has become tainted by something else in the basket.'

'Shall I still eat it. Mrs Thomas?'

'No, give it to Rags. I will fetch you out another.'

Edward knew his shaggy dog was in the stable yard greeting the doctor whose open carriage had just bowled down the drive. He ran from the kitchen door, round the side of the house, and across to the stables.

The pungent smell of hot horses and stable dung greeted him. The weather had set fair and Rowely Court was basking in the warmth.

'Papa, Papa, I have a gingerbread man for Rags,' he shouted when he spotted the tall dark man, talking to the doctor, dressed casually in buff breeches and white shirt, his boots dusty from the yard. Of his navy serge topcoat there was no sign.

'Do not shout, please Edward, where are your manners, lad?'

The boy skidded to a halt grinning up at both men. 'Good afternoon, Dr Witherspoon. Have you called to see my mother?'

'Yes, Edward, but I am told that she is resting, so I will not disturb her today.'

Edward crouched down and waved the treat in front of the dog's wet nose. 'I have something lovely for you, Rags. You are a hero, and you deserve it.'

Oliver raised an eyebrow. 'You are indeed honoured, Rags, I know these are your master's favourite.'

Edward watched his beloved companion gulp down the biscuit, his plumy tail wagging enthusiastically. 'I gave it to him, Papa, because Mrs Thomas and I thought it smelled nasty.'

Oliver acted instantly. Too late he dived down and forced the dog's jaws open, desperately hoping he had not swallowed the whole. Rags gave a groan and snatched his head away and tried to bite at his mid-section. Then his long legs buckled and he collapsed, writhing in agony, on the cobbles.

91

The doctor joined him on the around. 'Poison?'

Oliver nodded, his face grim. 'I realized too late. This is my fault. It could have been Edward.' He heard the boys smothered sob and his heart shrivelled. He had promised to protect this boy, and his mother, and now he had allowed his pet to be poisoned in front of him.

David Witherspoon had other ideas. 'There might still be time to save him. I need salt from the kitchen. Run fast Edward and fetch me a cupful.' Edward needed no further urging: he vanished. 'Get him up on his feet, and try to hold him steady.'

Oliver struggled with the writhing, whining dog, not wishing to cause him any more distress. He straddled Rags and, when the animal was more or less on his feet, he closed his knees and gripped hard. By the time Edward returned the doctor had a hollow glass tube and funnel ready. The salt was crushed into powder and stirred into enough water to make a liquid.

'Can you force his jaws apart and hold them open?'

Oliver nodded. With difficulty he tipped the dying dog's head hack and held his mouth open. David forced the glass tube down the dog's throat and slotted the funnel into the top. 'Edward, can you tip the salt water down for me, please?'

With shaking hands, and tear-stained cheeks, Edward bravely stepped up and slopped the solution into the open end of the funnel. It took the combined strength of both men to hold Rags still. The animal's body was convulsed in agony and Oliver believed that their actions were far too late.

'Good boy, that is enough. Now, you go in and sit with Sally. We will send for you when there is any news.'

Edward ignored the doctor's words and Oliver felt the small body pressed against his hip, seeking a comfort he could not deny. 'You can stay, but I warn you it will not be pleasant viewing.' Edward didn't answer, just pressed harder and Oliver felt little hands hanging onto his breeches.

For a moment nothing happened. A circle of grooms had gathered; everyone loved the big boisterous dog and all knew how much he meant to Edward. Then Rags's body convulsed and there was a horrible gurgling noise. The contents of his stomach began to be projected forcefully onto the cobbles. The miserable retching continued and the anxious watchers all saw that in the noxious pile large pieces of gingerbread were visible.

Oliver glanced up and his worried eyes met those of the doctor who said quietly, 'Possibly – it is too soon to say.'

The dog was now unconscious, but thankfully no longer squirming in desperate pain. Oliver gently lowered him to the ground. 'Run to the kitchen, Edward, and tell Mrs Thomas what has happened. Tell her we are going to bring Rags in so she will need to prepare a place for him, somewhere quiet and cool.'

Edward released his compulsive hold and sniffed loudly. 'Will Rags die, Papa?' His voice was little more than a whisper.

'I do not know, lad. We must pray that he does not. Now, hurry ahead: Rags needs you to be strong.' He gave the boy a hard hug and pushed him towards the archway. When he was out of earshot he turned to David. 'What chance is there?'

The doctor shrugged and ran his hand down the dog's chest, towards the shoulder, searching for a pulse. 'We have done all we can. He will have ingested a certain amount of the poison and his eventual recovery will depend how much that was.'

Oliver fondled the limp ears. 'He is young and strong, he will fight, I am sure of it.' His head dropped and he scowled. 'He must get better; Edward will be devastated if he dies. The animal is like a brother to him.'

The doctor replaced his apparatus in a battered leather bag. 'Can you manage the dog?'

Oliver nodded. 'Yes, thank you.' He was determined to do

so: this catastrophe was his fault, it was his responsibility to take care of things. He crouched and lifted the inert body. Leaning back, for balance, he straightened his legs and staggered upright. With the dog cradled in his arms he followed Edward, and the doctor, to the house, hoping Mrs Thomas had responded quickly and the necessary preparations had been made. When Rags was settled would be time enough to consider the implications of the incident.

His arms were aching by the time he reached the kitchen. The housekeeper had prepared a corner in the boot-room. Two clean blankets were ready to receive the deadweight. Gratefully he lowered the dog, which still showed no visible signs of life. Edward watched with tearful eyes as the dog's head flopped limply onto the hastily prepared bed.

'Can I stay here and look after him? He will want me to be with him when he wakes up.'

Oliver hesitated, realizing he was being asked a question best answered by Sarah. 'You will need your mother's approval, Edward. Shall we go up and ask her?'

The boy nodded and scrambled back to his feet. In silence the duo went up the backstairs that led from the servants' hall. Oliver was dreading the moment when he had to tell Sarah her attackers had once more breached his defences.

'Will she be awake, do you think, Papa?'

'Yes, I am sure she will be. And if she is not, then we will wake her.'

Beth's sombre face when she opened the bedchamber door meant the horrid news had already arrived. 'Madam is at her toilette, sir. She has asked if you will wait in her sitting-room. She won't be but a moment more.'

Oliver nodded and, still holding Edward's hand, took him to wait. 'It appears that your mother has already been told what has happened, Edward. Shall we sit down? Would you like me to tell you about my experiences at the Battle of Talevera?'

Normally such an offer would have been received with enthusiasm but Edward shook his head and to Oliver's surprise climbed onto his lap. The boy's head nestled into his shoulder trustingly, and he felt the slender form shudder. Instinctively he tightened his arms, his chest constricted with an alien emotion. Murmuring words of love and encouragement he lowered his head and kissed the grubby, tear-stained face. Neither of them heard the connecting door open softly or saw Sarah standing, framed in the sunlight, watching.

Her eyes brimmed and she knew, in that instant, that her decision was made. The love between Edward and Oliver was such that it made a marriage not only possible, but essential. It would be intolerable for her son to lose a father for a second time.

Oliver sensed her presence and looked up. Their eyes met and he mouthed, 'He is sleeping.'

Sarah mimed that he should put Edward down on the daybed and he did so, strangely unwilling to relinquish his burden. She beckoned and he followed her quietly into the window embrasure where they could talk without disturbing the child.

Everything had changed. Without conscious thought Sarah stepped forward and Oliver opened his arms and drew her close. She rested her head and could hear the sound of his heart beneath his soiled white shirt. Whatever their differences they must put them aside: Edward's welfare came first. She stepped away, but left her hand in his.

'Oliver, before we talk about the dog, there is something I wish to ask you.' She waited for him to acknowledge her unspoken request for permission to continue. He closed his hand, hard, around hers and nodded, his eyes gleaming and his expression watchful. 'Edward loves you and you love him. I know you will make him a wonderful father. I have been thinking and have decided that I would like our arrangement to become a real one. It would be advantageous to both of us. You would become wealthy and Edward and I would have a man to protect us. Would this be acceptable to you?'

In answer, Oliver dropped her hand and, his face alight with amusement, dropped dramatically to one knee. 'Sarah, will you do me the inestimable honour of becoming my wife?'

Sarah responded in kind and sank into a graceful curtsy. 'Oh, la, Captain Mayhew, this is so sudden! But yes, I will marry you.'

Oliver clasped his hands to his chest. 'You have made me the happiest of men, my angel.' He sprang to his feet and they both sobered. 'When do you wish to be wed, Sarah?'

'Soon. Perhaps at the beginning of July, that will give me six weeks to prepare.'

'Very well. Shall I arrange the details of the service with the vicar, or do you wish your father to perform the ceremony?'

'No, I wish him to escort me this time; he conducted the service between Jonathan and I. So, yes, please do speak to the vicar. I will write to my father and sister.' It was only then she remembered that her sister had yet to reply to her request for information about Oliver. Well, it was too late now. Whatever Elspeth might have discovered, the decision was made.

She glanced across at her son, exhausted by his grief. 'At least Edward will have something happy to look forward to.' She left unsaid the unpleasant fact that her son was likely to have to face the death of his closest companion. The news from downstairs was that Rags was sinking fast.

Chapter Ten

SALLY took her place beside her charge, allowing Sarah and
Oliver to descend to the study where they had matters of
importance to discuss. If Sarah was surprised to see the
young doctor still in evidence she disguised it well.

'We must thank you for your prompt action, Dr
Witherspoon. If you had not been here Rags would certainly
have died an agonizing death.'

'The animal is still gravely ill, Mrs Haverstock; the result
could still be death. I hope your little boy understands.'

'He does; we all do.'

'I remained solely to discuss what you can expect to
happen in the next few hours.' Sarah and Oliver nodded. 'The
dog will either slip away or he will regain consciousness. If he
does he will need careful nursing. Small amounts of boiled
water must be spooned into his mouth as often as he will take
them.'

'If he recovers, will there be lasting damage?'

'No, Mrs Haverstock, I think not.' He bowed to both of
them. 'I will take my leave. Please do not hesitate to send for
me.'

The door closed behind the doctor leaving them alone. She
stared, sniffed and, in spite of the circumstances, her mouth
curved. 'I do not believe I ever sat down with such a disrep-
utable figure.' He glanced, cursorily, at his stained shirt and
vomit spattered breeches. 'Good God! I cannot remain with

you like this.' He stood up, ready to rush off and repair the discrepancies of his attire.

Sarah shook her head, exasperated. 'Sit down, Oliver, it is far too late to worry. I have become used to the smell now.'

Grinning, he resumed his seat, but more carefully, trying to keep his stinking garments from the upholstery. Once settled he turned to her, his face serious. 'Somehow the enemy was able to substitute the poisoned gingerbreads. I have to discover how this was done.'

'It was not a member of Harriet's staff. I can assure you of that. They are all members of long standing and totally loyal.'

'Then the switch took place at a later stage. It worries me that Edward's taste for gingerbread was known. Someone close to you is giving away information.'

Sarah frowned, upset by the suggestion that any of her people were trying to harm Edward or herself. 'But all the girls who work in the house have been with me for several years.'

'And the outside men?'

'They also. Even Jack has worked here for three years.'

It was Oliver's turn to frown. 'Whoever it is had the information from someone.' He scowled, deep in thought, and Sarah watched him. Even in rank clothing, and with his hair unkempt, she could not help noticing that he was an attractive man. 'Of course! How could I not have thought of this? You have a household of unmarried young women. How many are walking out with lads from the village, do you know?'

'Jane and Sally are both courting local young men; they will be leaving to be married next spring, but how is that information of assistance?'

'Do any of them ever meet at the inn?'

'Yes, Sally does. Her fiancé is the son of the innkeeper.' Then she understood where the questions were leading. 'I see. Sally might well have discussed Edward on her visits and been overheard.'

'Exactly, I will send Jenkins to the inn and he can make discreet enquiries. I am afraid the informant has to be local, Sarah. I would know at once if there were strangers in the vicinity.'

It was inconceivable that someone who lived in her demesne could betray her to a murderer, but there was no other explanation. 'I agree: it can only be a local, no one else would have the necessary knowledge or be able to remain here unremarked.' Her woebegone face and slumped shoulders prompted Oliver to leave his seat to comfort her. At her involuntary recoil he stopped and grinned.

'I really must bathe and change. The smell is making me gag and I am used to far worse, as you can imagine.'

Sarah stood; her legs were so weak that, for a dreadful moment, she thought she would collapse. She surreptitiously gripped the chair back, hoping he would not notice.

'You are feeling unwell again – stay – I will carry you up.'

She wrinkled her nose. 'No, thank you. It was but a moments dizziness. I am fully recovered now. I will have Beth come down and assist me.'

Satisfied, he nodded. 'I will speak to Jenkins and send Jack with a note for Lord Hepworth. When I have some answers, shall I come and see you?' Both remembered what had transpired last time they had been alone together.

Sarah inclined her head. 'Please do, Oliver. I am eager to know how the substitution was undertaken without the delivery boy being aware of it.'

'So am I. I promise I will share any information as soon as I receive it.' Beth arrived and Oliver now felt free to leave. 'Your mistress has overtaxed herself. Beth. She will need your assistance on the stairs.' He glanced at Sarah and they smiled. The maid's expression of distaste on seeing him had not gone unnoticed.

*

Edward was still asleep and the longer he remained so the better. Sarah prayed that when he awoke the news from downstairs would be more encouraging. She dismissed his nursemaid knowing that she would be close by.

'I will not retire, Beth. I will rest on the *chaise-longue* in here.'

Beth fussed around, arranging pillows and fetching lavender water to bathe Sarah's forehead. When she had her mistress settled to her satisfaction, she withdrew to the dressing-room to continue with her mending. Sarah loved her maid dearly, but sometimes her solicitude was wearing. Left at last in blessed peace, she was able to relax and review the extraordinary events of the day.

The unknown assassin had tried to poison Edward and almost succeeded and now poor Rags lay fighting for his life. In spite of the cordon of riflemen, and the elaborate precautions to stop him, he had still been able to get close. Icy tremors shook her. For an instant her fear almost overwhelmed her and she pressed her fingers against her mouth to prevent a cry of anguish from escaping.

What was happening to them? A month ago she had been a happy woman, with neither financial nor any other worries. Now there had been three attempts on Edward's life and one on hers. She was no longer in control of her own destiny and was once more dependent on a man.

Indeed that very afternoon she had brazenly proposed marriage to a virtual stranger based on what? That he was a suitable match and would bring financial stability to the union? No – she had suggested they married because Oliver loved her son and could protect them both. Was this sufficient compatibility on which to base a lifetime's commitment?

It was far too late to repine. She would not renege on her promise now. It was her choice; it was a marriage of convenience and would be advantageous for them both. He, once a penniless, half-pay captain, would now be a rich man with extensive estates to manage. She would have a handsome husband to share her bed and father her children and Edward would have the father he had always wanted. She picked up the polished brass bell and rang it, once. 'Beth, I need pen and paper from my escritoire.'

Sarah was halfway through the second letter, this one to her sister, when Edward began to stir. She put her work aside and swung her legs to the floor. This time they did not betray her and she was able to walk briskly across to perch beside her son. She wished she had better news for him.

'Darling, have you had a lovely nap? I expect you will not wish to retire early tonight, so you may come down and eat with us, as a special treat.'

He beamed, momentarily forgetting about his pet. 'Thank you, Mama, I should like that.' Then his face fell and his mouth twisted with misery. 'Rags! I must go down and see him. Is he getting better? Please tell me he is better.'

'I wish I could, my dear. But he is no worse. Rags is young and strong and he will not give in easily.' She straightened his rumpled shirt and pushed his silky, black hair back from his eyes. 'Come along then, Edward, we will go down together and see how he does.'

They met Oliver on his way up and for a second her heart sank. Then she saw that his face, although serious, did not have the expression of someone bringing them dire news.

Edward released his vice-like grip and flew into his future father's outstretched arms. 'Papa, how is Rags? Have you been to see him?'

'I have, son, and he is a little better, I believe. Come and see for yourself.' He scooped Edward up and, carrying him easily, retraced his steps. Sarah followed behind, not sure she was glad Oliver was taking his new responsibilities so seriously or put out that her son appeared to prefer his company to her own.

Oliver ducked his head as he entered the boot-room. The

rear of the building, which housed the servants' quarters and offices, was of much older origins than the front, and constructed for smaller folk. He gently lowered the boy to his feet beside the inert dog. To their astonishment the long tail thumped in a feeble greeting. Edward fell to his knees and buried his face in the dog's smelly coat. The sick animal, still too weak to raise his head, attempted to lick Edward's cheek and his tail wagged twice more.

Sarah stretched out her hand and Oliver gripped it hard. She needed no urging to move closer, to feel his warm heavy arm encircle her shoulders and hold her safe. She felt both joy and relief flooding through her. Once again her fervent prayers had been answered. Their troubles were not over, not whilst the unseen enemy was still out there plotting, but she believed that her Lord was taking care of them.

The man so close beside her, sharing her delight at the dog's recovery, must have been sent to protect them. Her precipitate decision to make the union real was not a grave error of judgement but was clearly an action directed by the Almighty.

Sarah felt light-headed – giddy with relief – no longer plagued by doubts for, by convincing herself that God was guiding her actions, she could stop worrying that she might be marrying Oliver for all the wrong reasons. It would now be possible to start looking forward to their forthcoming nuptials. She sighed and rested her cheek against his pristine jacket.

'Sarah?'

She tipped her head to receive his kiss. Edward sat back and grinned at the interesting spectacle of his mother and future father exchanging a long embrace.

'Mama, Papa, Rags is better. Come and see.'

Reluctantly they stepped apart to join the child on the floor. The dog, despite his weakness, basked in their combined attention. His huge brown eyes shone in adoration and his tail renewed its thumping.

Sarah stroked the dog's head. 'Lie still, Rags, you must not over-exert yourself.'

'I expect he is pleased to see us all. I think he was lonely with only Elsie to take care of him, Mama.'

Oliver glanced across at the little scullery-maid, who had been designated nurse, and smiled broadly. 'You have done well, Elsie. We are grateful to you. Has the dog managed to swallow any water yet?'

The girl, her white apron mired and hair covered, smiled shyly at the huge, somewhat intimidating man. 'Yes, sir, that he has. Not at first, mind, but just before you came by, he fair gobbled it down off the spoon.'

'Good girl, you shall have an extra day off and a crown for your diligence.' Sarah told her. Elsie's face almost split with happiness.

'Thank you, madam. It is my grandma's name day next week: could I take that day off, if you please?'

Sarah nodded. 'Of course, you must. And have Cook pack you a basket to take with you as a gift.'

Edward, with guidance, had been spooning cool water into the dog's open mouth. Then fatigued by so much activity Rags closed his eyes and fell asleep. Edward gasped in horror, believing his dog had lapsed into unconsciousness again. Oliver squeezed the boy's shoulder reassuringly.

'Do not worry, Edward. He is only sleeping. Look, see how his chest is moving? He needs to rest now, but I promise you, he will be as good as new by the morning.'

'I will sit with him all night, Master Edward, don't you fret. If he needs anything, I'll be right here to fetch it.'

'Thank you, Elsie.' Edward ran forward and hugged the girl. 'Rags and I will always remember how you took care of him.'

Chatting happily, Edward led the way back through the narrow passageways, upstairs to his usual domain. He went willingly to find Sally, who was waiting in the freshly scrubbed nursery, on the understanding that he would be sent for when it was time to dine. The adults needed to converse, in private.

Oliver closed the study door and waited politely for Sarah to seat herself. 'I have discovered how the substitution was made, but not, unfortunately by whom it was done.'

'Tell me, how did they do it?'

'An under-footman was sent, in a pony cart, to deliver several parcels to various deserving cases in the village. He came here last. The cart was left unattended whilst he delivered the baskets. It would have been possible to exchange the gingerbread at any one of those stops.'

'And no one saw anything? One would think a stranger rummaging in Lord Hepworth's pony cart might have been noticed. Good heavens, there are more gossips in this village than anywhere else in England.'

He chuckled. 'Unfortunately they must all have been looking elsewhere today. I have also discovered that Edward's passion for gingerbread men is well known. It appears he would always gravitate to the cake stall at any village fair.'

'It is quite true. I should have thought of that for myself.' She smiled. 'At least we no longer need to suspect anyone of betraying us. That is a relief.'

'I have also spoken to the Reverend Murray. He is naturally overjoyed at our news and will arrange to have the banns called. Have you your letters written?'

'Almost. I will finish them before dinner and Jack can take them over to Hepworth House. It is a good thing the nights are lighter now, I would not wish him to be out in the dark.'

Sarah closed her eyes for a moment, lost in thought. If she was to be married in six weeks she would have to meet with her lawyers immediately. Once the vows were spoken she would no longer have control of her properties or money, all of it would become her husband's responsibility. She had to take the necessary steps to protect both Edward's and her own financial future in the unlikely event that Oliver should turn out to be a gambler, or worse.

She sat up. She must go to London as soon as possible. He could pursue his enquiries more easily in the capital and she could get her financial affairs in order. 'I intend to travel to town, as soon as I am declared well enough. Edward can accompany me.'

The announcement was greeted with incredulity. 'Have you run mad, Sarah? There is a maniac on the loose and you want to leave the safety of your home?'

'I believe we will be as safe, or perhaps safer, away from here. If your riflemen come with us we will be well protected on the journey. Surely it will be harder for the person to get near to us in town?'

Oliver scowled. He was unused to having his movements dictated by another person. He expected to be in command at all times. 'Why do you wish to travel now? Why not wait until we have discovered why someone wishes you dead?'

'I have to see my lawyers and it will not wait. And I am sure it will be easier for you to speak to your investigators in person rather than relying on written messages.'

He stared at Sarah, his eyes narrowed, his expression hard. 'I know why you wish to see your lawyers. You are protecting your assets, are you not? You do not trust me to use your fortune wisely.'

Sarah felt revealing colour flush her cheeks. She stood up, embarrassment and guilt making her speak unwisely. 'Yes, of course that is why I am going. Do you blame me? I know nothing of you, apart from what you have told me. How would Lady Hepworth feel if I allowed Edward's fortune to be gambled away?'

'God's teeth!' Oliver swore, his manners forgotten. 'If that is how you feel why in God's name are you marrying me?'

Sarah tried to remain composed in the face of his anger. 'I

am doing so because Edward loves you and you will make him an excellent father. And I do not wish him to remain an only child.'

The force with which the door slammed behind him almost lifted her from her feet.

Chapter Eleven

THE silence that followed Oliver's explosive exit gave Sarah time to gather her scattered wits. Should she run after him and apologize or let him recover his temper first? Undecided, she paced the room, the speed of her passage swirling her skirts and threatening to remove the newspapers from the desktop.

Then she stopped. She had quite forgotten that they had promised Edward he could join them for dinner. She had never broken her word to her son and would not do so now. Swallowing hard, with clammy palms but straight back, she hurried from the room in search of her intended. She met Jack in the hallway.

'Have you seen the captain, Jack? I wish to speak to him.'

Jack's face went pale. 'I have, madam, but he is in a fearful temper. He near scared me half to death when he went past.'

'I am not asking you to find him, Jack. I merely wish to know where he is at this moment.'

Relieved, the youth smiled nervously. 'He was heading for the Dower House and the speed he was moving I reckon he is there by now.'

Sarah frowned. Should she risk further exacerbating the situation by defying his explicit orders not to leave the house, or disappoint her son? She had no choice. 'Are the riflemen about, Jack?'

'Yes, madam, they are all over the park.'

'Excellent. I am going to the Dower House, would you fetch Sam from the stables, you shall both accompany me.' With Sam from the stables, and Jack, and the riflemen in the woods, she should be safe enough.

Jack ran off to fetch the under-groom and Sarah returned to her room to change from her slippers to stout boots. The walk was over a mile and she had no desire to acquire blisters on her journey.

Her escorts were waiting for her on the drive when she returned. Determined to complete the walk in as short a time as possible, Sarah set off at a brisk pace. She had travelled scarcely one hundred yards when she heard running feet approaching.

'Excuse me, madam. You must not go in there.' Two neatly dressed men, carrying well serviced rifles, halted with military precision beside her.

'I am going to the Dower House. It is imperative that I speak with Captain Mayhew immediately.'

The taller man stepped politely in front of her. 'I'm sorry, madam, we have our orders. You are to stay within sight of the house at all times. If you return I will send a runner to fetch the captain back.'

Sarah admitted defeat. 'Very well. But please stress to the captain how important it is he returns at once.'

Sarah heard the man whistle and a third, younger, but equally well-armed ex-soldier, trotted up, nodded and jogged off down the path she had been about to take herself.

There was no more she could do. She doubted that Oliver, in his present frame of mind, would answer her summons to return.

Oliver was not at the Dower House, he had changed his mind and doubled back, cutting through the woods, and was venting his spleen by hurling stones into the lake. The satisfactory splashes began to have the desired effect and slowly his choler dissipated. He gazed morosely across the sparkling water watching the offended water-birds slowly return to their positions bobbing on the surface.

His mind was in a turmoil. He could not understand why he became so enraged by Sarah's idiotic outbursts. She was a woman, after all, and in his limited experience of the fairer sex he had not found them particularly rational in their outlook. His objective had been achieved; he had taken the position at Rowley Court with the express intention of charming Sarah into marriage. Did it really matter that she had pre-empted him?

He smiled. He understood now how the new debutantes must feel as they were paraded, like brood mares, by their ambitious mothers at Almack's every season. It was not a comfortable feeling being selected for one's breeding qualities.

He yawned and ran his hand idly down his jaw, glad this evening that he would not need to shave again, as he had no intention of dining with Sarah. Then he remembered the promise to Edward and swore. He kicked viciously at a boulder. The resulting agony that shot down his injured toes made him swear again. He was a man who kept his word and knew he would have to swallow his pride and return to the house. He stamped his damaged foot experimentally and his austere features relaxed into a grin. He supposed he must get used to taking solitary promenades if he was to shackle himself to Sarah. But woe betide her if she angered him again today: he would not be answerable for the consequences!

He was strolling back when he saw two of his men approaching at the double. His stomach lurched. The dog had died, it could be nothing else, and Sarah could not bear to break the news to Edward. He broke into a run and met the riflemen halfway.

'Out with it, Smith. What has happened?

'Mrs Haverstock wishes to speak with you urgently, sir. We

intercepted her on her way to the Dower House. We have been searching for you this past half-hour, Captain.'

Oliver continued at a run, dreading the task before him. He loved Edward and did not wish to see him hurt.

Sarah looked at the clock for the tenth time and resigned herself to the unpalatable fact that Oliver was not coming. Edward was going to be disappointed but it could not be helped. It was past time for her to return to her rooms and change. She had given Sally instructions to dress Edward in his best; she could do no less herself.

She was halfway up the stairway when she heard the side door crash open and booted feet thundering down the passage towards the study. Alarmed, she flew back down the stairs to the hall and ran, her skirts held high, heart pounding.

They arrived simultaneously at the study door. To avoid a collision Oliver was forced to halt so suddenly his feet shot forward in his boots and his injured toes were painfully squashed again. He barely managed to swallow his oath. He hobbled after Sarah into the study.

'I am so sorry, Sarah. Edward will be devastated.' Sarah's blank look made him pause. 'Rags? You sent for me because he has died.'

Sarah knew she was in trouble. She had made her summons unnecessarily urgent so it was small wonder he had made such an erroneous assumption.

'I am sorry. Oliver, there has been a misunderstanding. Rags is not dead. I only wished to remind you of your promise to dine with Edward tonight.' She shifted nervously and fiddled with her sash, unwilling to meet his eyes. She could hear him breathing heavily, but still the storm did not break over her bowed head. Puzzled, she risked a glance up and, to her astonishment, saw he was having difficulty containing his amusement.

'You are incorrigible, Sarah, my love. I am in two minds

whether to put you over my knee or . . .' His words died away and she saw the predatory gleam in his eye and felt her heart skip a beat.

She raised her hand, placatingly, not sure if she would prefer a spanking to the alternative he had in mind. Oliver reached out and her hand disappeared in his. Then she was yanked forward unceremoniously and all but fell into his waiting arms.

'You are a sore trial to me, my dear. What do you suggest I do about it?' His words were barely audible but sent a frisson of fear, or was it excitement, down her spine. Then, instead of the expected searing kiss, he laughed out loud and swung her round, making her head spin and her skirts swirl indecorously above her ankles. Replacing her, none too gently, on her feet, he stepped back, holding her at arm's length.

Thoroughly flustered Sarah watched him, unsure what he would do next. He grinned, enjoying her discomfiture. He gave her a little shake before dropping his hands. Sarah hastily put a chair between them before risking her reply.

'I am sorry if I misled you, Oliver, it was not my intention.'

'I am sure it was not,' he answered, his expression bland.

'I was frightened too, when I heard you racing down the passage.'

'Good, it was no more than you deserve. Your stupidity involved my men in unnecessary work and caused me to run all the way from the lake.'

Enough was enough! Sarah was indignant. 'Do not call me stupid. I am not one of your men to be so casually insulted.'

'You may be grateful you are not, my girl. I have had men flogged for less.' She did not see the glint in his eyes as he spoke.

She gasped. 'But that is disgraceful! How could you be so cruel?'

'Cut rope, Sarah. It was a joke. Do you honestly think I am the sort of officer who floggs his men?'

Shamefaced, Sarah blushed. 'Oh, no, of course not.' She quickly changed the subject. 'You are staying for dinner, are you not, Oliver?'

He groaned and turned, pretending to bang his head in frustration on the wall. Sarah stamped her foot equally exasperated. 'What is the matter with you, Oliver? You are behaving like a child. He turned back to face her, shaking his head and tutting at her in the most annoying way. 'If you do not desist, I will strike you,' she shouted at him, her patience at an end.

He stepped in, fast, until he was a hand's width away. 'Go ahead, Sarah. But I warn you I will retaliate.'

Sarah felt the heat pulsing from him and every instinct urged her to retreat. But she could not: her feet remained rooted to the floor. Instead she tipped her head, rested her hands on his shoulders, stretched up and pressed a soft kiss on his parted lips. Before he could react she skipped out of reach and he heard her tinkling laughter as she ran back along the corridor and away upstairs to change for dinner.

Tentatively he ran his tongue over his lips and tasted the sweetness she had left behind. 'God damn it! That woman is as random as a weather-vane!' He shook his head in disbelief that, once again, he had been wrong-footed and his intended bride had taken the honours. He stomped off, surly as a schoolboy but already his quick wits were plotting her comeuppance. Reluctantly he felt a bubble of mirth fighting to escape and chuckling to himself he bounded up the steps two at time.

It was then he admitted he was enjoying his regular spats with Sarah. Indeed he was already eagerly anticipating their next encounter. At least being married to such a woman his life would never be dull.

Dinner *à trois* was a great success. Oliver sat at the head of the table, Edward to his right, Sarah to his left. Cook presented a simple repast prepared especially for Edward's childish palate. By the last remove of sugared fruit, a blanc-manger and a bowl of sliced pineapple from Lord Hepworth's hothouse, Edward was visibly wilting.

'It is time for you to go up, my love. Sally is waiting to put you to bed.'

'Yes, Mama. Thank you for allowing me to stay.' His head nodded and his elbow slipped from the table noisily.

'I will carry him up. He is asleep on his feet.' Oliver did not wait for her consent. He pulled Edward's chair back and lifted him. 'I will join you in the drawing-room. Do not go up: I wish to talk to you.'

He was gone, her son in his arms as though he owned him, before Sarah could answer. She was sorely tempted to ignore his words and creep off to bed but did not trust him not to follow her and she well knew where such a visit could lead.

She drifted from the table into the connecting drawing-room. The terrace windows were still open and the room was pleasantly cool. The lamps were lit and made pretty pools of golden light on the surfaces upon which they rested. Sarah had no candles downstairs believing oil-lamps were safer when there was a child in the house.

She paused in front of the mantle to adjust the *décolletage* of her dinner-gown. She pushed a stray strand of hair back into the simple chignon she wore at the base of her neck. She stared at her reflection critically. Did she look any different, for she believed she must? Her blood seemed to be fizzing round her veins; she had never felt so alive. Danger was obviously agreeing with her.

Her eyes sparkled with excitement and the embroidered bodice of her russet silk gown felt tight and made her long to remove it and replace it with something less restrictive. Not wishing to be caught preening at the mirror she walked down the handsome room and out onto the terrace. The moon was small and the night dark. She saw a flicker of movement by the yew hedge that made her jump.

A cheerful voice called out. 'Good evening, Mrs Haverstock. Lovely night.'

Relieved, she replied 'Good evening, Jenkins. Are you stationed there all night?'

'Yes, madam. There will be someone here until dawn.'

Light footsteps approaching from behind her indicated that Oliver was back. She spoke without turning. 'When do the men sleep, if they are working both day and night?'

'They have six hours on, six off. That way I always have enough men on duty.' He answered from a position so close behind her she felt the hairs on the back of her neck tingle. She stepped forward but he followed and this time he put his arms around her slender waist and held her lightly, making further movement impossible.

'Stop fighting me, sweetheart. You are to be my bride in a few weeks. It is time we got to know each other more intimately.' As he was speaking he slowly tightened his arms until she was pressed hard against his chest.

His logic was unanswerable. If she was to share her body with him soon, a few kisses could hardly matter, so why should she not relax and enjoy it? She leant into his embrace, loving the feel of his hard legs behind her.

'You are right, Oliver, I am being missish. It is not as though such things are new to me, after all.'

The reminder that Sarah had once belonged to another man did not please Oliver. All desire to make love to her instantly evaporated. He ran his hands insolently over her breasts before removing them. Back rigid, he vanished inside leaving Sarah feeling embarrassed and humiliated. She shook her head crossly and then followed him, intending to demand an explanation.

However, the room was empty. He had gone. Whatever he had once intended to say to her was obviously not that important. She rang for Mrs Thomas. She would retire but first she had some plans to make. The housekeeper came bustling in.

'I intend to go to town, Mrs Thomas. Can you send ahead and have the house made ready for a visit?'

'When are you expecting to leave, madam?'

'The day after tomorrow. The roads are dry and, if we set out early, we will be in London by the evening.'

'Very well, madam. I will go myself, tomorrow and sort things out. It must be two years since we were there and no doubt the staff have allowed things to slip in your absence.'

'Good. Captain Mayhew and Edward will be accompanying me, of course. And accommodations will have to be made for the extra men who will be travelling with us.'

'You will be taking Beth and Sally, I expect, madam.'

'Of course, and you had better take two of the parlourmaids with you. You will need the extra staff.'

'Do you intend to entertain, madam?'

'No, the season is almost over.'

'In that case we will have enough staff to manage. Will that be all, Mrs Haverstock?'

'I am going to retire. You can lock up after me.'

'Captain Mayhew has gone out again. I will need to wait up for him. Goodnight, madam.' Sarah waited for the door to close behind the housekeeper before allowing her annoyance to escape. 'Drat the man! He has no right to keep my staff up; he is most inconsiderate.'

'How very kind of you to say so, my love.' The deep voice that spoke from the terrace so startled her she dropped the oil-lamp she had picked up to light her way to the bedroom.

She screamed as the oil spilled and the flames flicked greedily at her skirt hem. Then she was on the floor, being rolled furiously inside the Persian rug. Seconds later she was free and sobbing with frightened relief against Oliver's chest.

'Hush, darling. It is over. You are unhurt. The fire is out.'

But Sarah was shaking so much she was almost incapable

of answering. 'If you had not been there, I should have been burnt alive.'

In answer he carried her to the nearest chair and sat down, cradling her close to his heart. 'My love, if I had not been here, the accident would not have happened in the first place.'

Chapter Twelve

THE aftermath of the second fire was not as disastrous as the first. It involved no more than a ruined dress, a broken oil-lamp and burnt rug. It also repaired the rift in Oliver and Sarah's relationship and they parted, that night, on excellent terms. He wished they had not parted at all.

This accident had revealed to him a startling fact. He had avoided becoming entangled with hopeful young ladies and falling into the parson's mousetrap for his entire adult life. Finally, at two and thirty, not only was he approaching his marriage willingly, but also he had actually fallen in love with his future wife.

When he had seen Sarah with flames at her feet he had known that if he lost her, his life would have no meaning. She was his heart, the very breath he breathed. As he stripped off his smoke-damaged evening-shirt he considered just how his change of feeling was going to alter his life.

Before his affections had become engaged he had been quite content to marry Sarah on her terms: be a father to Edward, manage the estates and provide her with the babies she craved to fill the empty nursery. This was no longer going to be possible. Loving Sarah meant he needed her to love him in return. Without this, making love to her would not be possible and he decided that he would no longer be able to fulfil his side of the bargain.

There were still six weeks to the wedding. Perhaps that was

time enough to woo his wayward bride into admitting that she loved him. One thing was certain: he would not reveal his true feelings until he was sure that Sarah returned them.

Sarah came out to watch the carriages, taking their baggage and Mrs Thomas and the parlour-maids to London, prepare to leave. 'Edward, Rags cannot come with us. He is still too weak; the heat and noise would make him ill again.'

'But, Mama, he will pine on his own. I have left him for a single night, never a whole week.'

Sarah ruffled his hair. 'Elsie will take good care of him. He loves her too, does he not?' She watched Sam and Jack load the last trunk into the baggage cart. The housekeeper and the two girls clambered into the ancient carriage. Edward was distracted by the activity and wandered off to say his farewells to Sam, who was driving the carriage, and Jack who had been promoted to under-groom.

The two vehicles rattled out of the yard. She felt the warm weight of Rags against her leg. 'How are you, boy? Still too tired to run after Edward, but never mind, you will be back to normal soon enough.' The dog thumped his tail and pressed harder, leaving her delicate, muslin morning-gown liberally covered with dog hairs. Sarah didn't care. Like all the household she was so glad the dog had not died that he now had *carte blanche* to behave as he wished. Ruefully she had acknowledged that her son's pet would now have a permanent position inside the house.

She had not spoken privately to Oliver that morning; for some reason whenever she approached he appeared to find urgent business in the opposite direction. For once her conscience was clear: she had done nothing that could possibly have offended him. Maybe she was imagining it, after all he had his men to organize and an estate to run.

The letters informing her father and her sister of the date of her forthcoming marriage had been dispatched. Mrs Thomas had been instructed to deliver a letter to her lawyers containing the details of her wishes with regard to the estate and her funds. The note also asked them to call on her at a specified time.

'Edward, I am going in. You will stay near the house, will you not? Remember what you have been told.' She still could not bring herself to refer to Oliver as Edward's father.

'Yes, Mama. Rags can not go far, and I will stay with him.'

The Hepworth's had sent word that they were intending to call that afternoon. Sarah feared the visit would revolve around her wedding plans. It was going to be difficult to lie to Harriet and pretend that it was a love match but she had no choice. Her friends would be horrified if they knew that not only had she proposed the match herself but also her reasons for so doing had nothing to do with love and everything to do with expediency and convenience.

It was imperative that she talked to Oliver before they arrived. It would not do for them to appear as anything other than besotted with each other. She giggled at the notion: he was a soldier to the core. The gentler emotions did not feature in his makeup. Passion and lust, yes, he had more than enough of that, but she was sure he was not capable of love.

Then she recalled the picture of her son being cradled lovingly and realized she was perhaps misjudging him. After all he did love her son. But a woman? She doubted he had ever seen a female as more than a warm body in the dark, to be used and discarded the next morning.

Sarah caught a fleeting glimpse of broad, blue serge covered shoulders and black top-boots but sensibly refrained from calling out: Oliver would inevitably vanish if she did so. She ran him to earth in the estate office at the back of the house.

'There you are Oliver. I have to speak to you.'

Resigned, he pulled out a plain wooden chair for her to sit on. 'If you must, my dear, I suppose I will have to listen.' He sounded so dejected at the prospect that Sarah forgot about her vow to remain polite in all circumstances.

'For heaven's sake, Oliver, what is the matter? You have a face as long as a wheelbarrow this morning. And you are trying to avoid me? There is no point in denying it, you know.'

His face was sober when he spoke. 'I have no intention of denying it, Sarah. I decided it was safer, for both of us, to remain as far from each other as possible. Good God, woman, my stupidity nearly caused your death last night. I am surprised you can bring yourself to speak to me.'

'Do not be so ridiculous. Your prompt action saved my life, something you appear to be making habit of, I might add.'

Slowly his mobile mouth curved and his eyes held a suspicious glitter. 'So, my love, I am both ridiculous and stupid. It is a miracle that you think I am capable of running this estate.'

Sarah's eyes twinkled in response. 'You are so right. I am momentarily considering placing it in Edward's capable hands.'

His smile flipped her heart over. 'I am serious, Sarah. Are you quite sure you wish to continue with all this?' He gestured vaguely around the room. 'I will quite understand if you wish to break the engagement.'

Sarah leant across the scratched pine table and placed her hands on his. 'Never! I am happy as things are.' She sat back and smiled. 'And anyway it is too late: I have told both my sister and my father and the banns are being called this Sunday.'

'Well, if you are sure, then I must give you this.' He reached into his waistcoat pocket and removed a small box, almost shyly, and dropped it into her hand. 'It was my grandmother's. She gave it to me on my majority.'

She undid the gold filigree clasp and flicked back the lid. 'Oh, Oliver! It is lovely!' She removed the exquisite ring and was about to slip it on, then paused, staring at her plain gold wedding band. She hesitated for an instant before slowly slipping it off her finger and dropping it into the empty box. And then she held the ring out to him and he took it and, holding her left hand, gently pushed the ring down her finger. It fitted as though it had been made for her.

Sarah eyed it with unfeigned delight. 'I love it. The setting is so intricate. The central emerald and the small golden stones all round it are quite beautiful.'

'The golden stones are topaz. The ring came originally from Persia, I believe, hundreds of years ago.' The removal of the wedding band and its replacement with the engagement ring was truly significant. By so doing Sarah had demonstrated to him that she was placing herself, and her son, in his hands.

They smiled, for once, in perfect accord. Sarah moved her hands and placed them firmly in her lap then resumed her usual brisk, impersonal manner. 'Oliver, exactly how have you organized this journey? Do your men travel as postilions or do they ride with you?'

'Jenkins and Smith, as the only two who can ride, will do so. Peters and Murray will ride on the coach. I will lead, of course.'

'I thought that Tom coachman and William, my headgroom, who are both experienced, should drive my carriage. They have faced footpads twice and on both occasions the accuracy of William's shots frightened them away.'

'In that case he is an excellent choice, although I do not anticipate there will be any trouble of that sort. I doubt that even our enemy would be foolhardy enough to attack a coach with six armed men accompanying it.'

Sarah nodded. 'I would not contemplate this journey if I thought I was placing Edward in danger.'

'At what time will you be ready to leave?'

'At six o'clock. I would like to accomplish the journey whilst it is still cool. Travelling becomes intolerable when the weather is hot.'

121

Oliver was pleased by her response. 'Excellent. I shall send the remaining men ahead to check the local lanes before we leave. Once we are on the toll road we must be safe from attack.'

Sarah pushed her chair hack. 'I am looking forward to this visit. It is two years since I was in town and Edward was far too young to remember much. I have promised him we will take him to see the Tower.'

'I shall look forward to that. When do you see your lawyers?' The enquiry was made without noticeable change of inflection, but she knew this aspect of her trip still rankled.

'I have asked them to attend me at the house on Thursday, at ten o'clock. This will leave ample time for any adjustments and alterations that I might require to be done and still leave time for the documents to be returned to me for signing, before we travel home.' Sarah ignored his sour expression. 'Have you any meetings planned with those who are searching the marriage records?'

'They are well able to search without interference from me. If they uncover the names we seek they will let me know immediately.' The atmosphere had now moved from pleasant to strained and she had no wish to out-stay her fragile welcome.

She stood up. 'Actually I came to tell you Lord and Lady Hepworth, and their daughters, will be coming this afternoon. They will expect to see you too.'

'And I shall not disappoint them.' He half bowed and she nodded and left. Oliver watched her walk gracefully away, her nut-brown hair almost russet in the sunlight. Their meeting had once more ended unsatisfactorily. It would seem that they were both incapable of remaining on good terms for more than a brief moment. And when she discovered that he had decided not to consummate the union it was not going to improve the situation between them.

*

Sarah, Oliver and Edward waited on the steps to greet the
Hepworths. Oliver had appeared at the last possible moment,
impeccably dressed in dark-grey top coat, crisp white shirt,
pale blue waistcoat and impressively tied neck cloth. His
breeches were fashionably skin-tight and his Hessians
restored to their original shine. He was the epitome of an
attentive bridegroom, a happy smile pinned securely to his
face. Only Sarah knew he was play-acting.

She had dressed with equal care in an afternoon-gown,
with a pale green underskirt, short capped sleeves and white
sarcenet overdress. She had had her hair dressed in a coronet
and Beth had threaded matching green ribbons through the
braid. Her left hand, new ring prominently displayed, rested
on the right arm of her fiancé. Edward was resplendent in
brown nankeen breeches and matching jacket. They made a
handsome picture, which did not go unremarked by their
visitors.

Lady Hepworth hurried forward to embrace Sarah. 'My
dear, I am so glad you have set a date. I have brought with me
some copies of *La Belle Assemblee*, which have but recently
arrived. There are several gowns depicted that would make
you a perfect wedding dress.'

Lord Hepworth shook Oliver heartily by the hand. 'Well
done, my boy. Just the ticket. Shall we leave the ladies to their
plans? I would like to hear, in person, about the latest atroci-
ties.' The party divided. Oliver and Lord Hepworth vanished
speedily to the study. Edward and his four young aunts led
the way noisily to the drawing-room where tea, hot scones
and cakes were to be served.

Sarah and Harriet followed more quietly, but equally
pleased to see each other. The girls ranged in age from Sophia
who was seventeen and about to make her curtsy to society,
to Lucinda who was ten, near enough Edward's age to be a
friend. Sophia joined Sarah and her mother by the tea-tray.
Her sisters and Edward lay across the carpet, a box of

123

spillikins scattered in front of them.

Harriet studied Sarah closely. 'Are you sure, my dear? It is a big step you are taking. Do not let my silly remarks, and the present difficult circumstances, push you into something you might later regret.'

'I am quite sure, thank you, Harriet. Oliver will make a wonderful father and a good husband.' She smiled and her eyes shone with sincerity. 'I have been on my own too long.'

Harriet, convinced, allowed her delight to show. 'He is perfect for you, my love. I could not have chosen better for you myself.'

Over light scones, sticky strawberry jam and Cook's own recipe fruitcake, the dresses were selected and the plans made. Charity, Chloe and Lucinda were delighted to be asked to be Sarah's flower-girls and walk ahead of her to the church, scattering rose petals on the path.

Harriet insisted that the wedding breakfast would be held at Hepworth House. As it was to be a small affair and immediate family only were attending, everyone could be accommodated easily under her roof. Although both Sarah and Harriet had not mentioned it, they knew that, unless the mystery surrounding the attempted assassinations was solved and the perpetrators unmasked, there would be no wedding. It would be far too dangerous.

Eventually the visit ended and they made their farewells. Lord Hepworth declared himself satisfied with the arrangements made for the journey to London and Lady Harriet and her daughters were delighted with the wedding plans.

Oliver stepped away from Sarah as soon as the coach was out of sight. 'I will not be joining you for dinner this evening, Sarah. I still have much to do.'

'In that case I will eat in my room. As we intend to leave at six o'clock we all need to retire early.'

Oliver refrained from pointing out that, as a soldier, he was used to functioning on less than three hour's sleep. 'Edward,

I will see you in the morning. Are you looking forward to your visit to London?'

The little boy beamed, unaware of the tension. 'I am. I have a book with pictures of the sites. I cannot wait to see them for myself.'

Oliver stoked Edward's hair, nodded to Sarah, and headed off towards the Dower House where his ten men were billeted. Sadly, Sarah returned to the drawing-room beginning to regret her decision to leave the familiar surroundings of Rowley Court and travel to Town in the company of the man who plainly wished to be anywhere but with her.

The early morning mist was still drifting between the trees and the lake when Sarah, Edward, Beth and Sally took their places in the smart, travelling coach. The four horses, chestnut coats gleaming, stamped impatiently, eager to be off.

The vehicle rocked alarmingly as the riflemen scrambled to their positions at the rear. Sarah heard the thump of their weapons as they were rested, primed and ready, on the roof. Then she saw Oliver emerge, mounted on a magnificent grey stallion and followed closely by Jenkins and Smith on sturdy bay hunters.

Edward hung, grinning, from the open carriage window. 'Papa, your horse looks just like my rocking horse, but fiercer and much much bigger.'

He rode over so that the child could pat the horses' iron-grey neck. 'Trojan is not fierce, lad, just strong and fit.' The animal, as if to prove the point, lowered his enormous head and rubbed it gently on Edward's face. The boy crowed with delight and returned the kiss.

Sarah had slid across the seat in order to speak to Oliver. 'Did your men discover anything amiss when they checked the lanes this morning?'

He shook his head. 'No, if they had I would have heard by

now. If you are ready I think we should get started, before the sun is fully up.'

'I have sent ahead to order refreshments to be served at the Red Lion. We will need to rest the horses and stretch our legs by then.'

Oliver frowned. 'I had hoped to complete the journey without stopping.'

Sarah chuckled at his disgruntlement. 'We are not soldiers on a route march, Oliver. Four hours cooped up in here is more than enough for us mere mortals.'

'Very well, as always, I will capitulate.' He grinned and swung the huge horse away. Tom coachman flicked his whip and, releasing the brake, the coach lurched forward. Oliver led the way and his mounted riflemen followed on behind. They were all alert and ready for a possible ambush.

None of them saw the watcher hidden in the trees slide furtively backwards, remount his horse and gallop off across the fields.

Chapter Thirteen

THE small cavalcade had been trundling slowly along the narrow leafy lane that led from the village to the busy toll road for almost an hour. Edward, not yet bored with the ride, bounced from one side of the carriage to the other, putting his head out of each window, treading on toes and twice knocking his mother's chip-straw bonnet over her eyes.

'That will do, Edward. Decide which side you wish to be seated and remain there. You are making us giddy with all your rushing around.'

Edward grinned. 'I will sit here, on the left of you. I promise not to move again, except for looking out of the window.'

'Good boy. Can you see Captain Mayhew ahead?'

'No, the lane is too windy.' He craned his head to look backwards. 'Neither can I see Jenkins or Murray, but I can hear them, I think.'

Suddenly the carriage rocked and the passengers were almost tipped from their seats as Tom wrenched the horses to a shuddering halt. Sarah's stomach clenched in dread. Then they heard the sound of sheep bleating all around them.

'The lane is full of woolly sheep, Mama, they are milling everywhere; we are quite surrounded by them!'

Unexpectedly Peters's face appeared at the window. 'Close the windows and pull down the blinds, quickly, please. Then all of you on the floor, between the seats, and stay there until I give you leave to move.' He waited until he was sure they were going to react then vanished.

Beth and Sally had instantly sunk to the protection of the floor well taking Edward, too surprised to protest, with them. This left Sarah to deal with the blinds and windows. Her hands were shaking so much she thought she would not be able to fasten them securely.

'But it is only sheep, how can they hurt us?' Edward whispered as she joined the cramped huddle on the floor.

'They could have been released deliberately to separate us from our protectors.' She wriggled, trying to release the skirts of her smart green travelling-dress from under her bottom. 'I am sure Peters is just being cautious, my love. It is what he is paid to do, after all.'

The inside of the carriage was not only plunged into semi-darkness but was becoming unbearably hot and stuffy. They were too squashed to be able to remove petticoats, but Sarah hastily tossed her bonnet onto the seat. The caps of both Beth and Sally soon followed.

After the initial burst of activity and noise it was eerily silent outside apart from the incessant bleating of the sheep. Sarah had heard Peters tell Tom the coachman and William to get down from the box, bringing their weapons with them. William had already done so but Tom was still aloft, securing the reins.

'Hurry up, Tom. You are an easy mark up there,' Peters hissed from his position on the ground at the rear of the coach.

'I'm done now. I do not want trouble with the horses. The ladies and the little lad are still inside, remember.'

Sarah heard a single gunshot, a single cry of agony and a loud thud as Tom fell to the ground. 'Tom has been shot. I have to go to him.' Sarah called.

Murray's rough voice answered. 'Stay put, madam. There is nothing you can do for Tom.'

His meaning was clear. Beth burst into noisy tears and Sally put her arms around her friend. Sarah's first concern was Edward. She gathered him close and rocked him like a baby.

'Tom will have felt no pain, Edward. He is in a better place now, in heaven with our Lord.'

Her son pulled his ashen face away and even in the darkness of the coach floor she could see his eyes were huge with horror. 'Are we all going to die? Is someone out there going to shoot us too?'

'No, Edward, we are safe in here. Tom was too slow getting down. If he had been on the ground like the others, he would have been safe.'

Her words were cut short as there was a flurry of shots. Two bullets thudded into the coach sides splintering the wood but causing no damage to those cowering inside. Peters and the other two returned fire and the acrid smell of cordite filtered into their small hidey-hole to add to their discomfort.

There was nothing Sarah could do to protect her son, apart from use her own body as a shield. The shots had come from the left of the coach so slowly she inched forward until she was leaning hard against that door. Then she pulled Edward into the space between her knees. It was the best she could do.

Beth, having quickly regained control of her grief, understood what her mistress was attempting to do. She shuffled across the floor until she was able to place her knees in front of Edward. Cradled between the two women he was as safe as it was possible to make him. Edward, hot between them, wriggled crossly.

'How long will we have to sit like this? It is too hot and cramped.'

'I know, my dear. But at least you are safe down here.'

Unexpectedly Edward smiled. 'It will not be for long. Papa is out there, so are Jenkins and Smith, they will soon sort out these villains.'

Sarah felt a wave of icy sickness. For a moment she had forgotten Oliver was somewhere, alone, facing God knows what. She prayed fervently that he would not meet the same horrid end as poor Tom.

Oliver heard the sheep blunder out of the field behind him and immediately understood their significance. He didn't wait for the ambush to be sprung, he hauled Trojan's head round and dug his heels into the horse's sides and sent it headlong at the five-barred gate at the side of the lane. Two strides were all the stallion had but it was enough: his massive hindquarters bunched and launched them into the air. He cleared the top rung with inches to spare.

They landed safely and Oliver urged the horse into a gallop. He had to get behind the attackers before they realized he had left the lane. He vaulted from the saddle whilst Trojan was still moving and rolled, rifle in one hand, into the undergrowth. The horse, startled by the sudden disappearance of his rider, bolted noisily past the copse where three men waited to complete the task they had been paid handsomely to do.

Trojan's passage convinced them that Oliver was approaching on horseback when in fact he was, at that very moment, crawling with deadly stealth through the undergrowth towards them. Oliver tensed and carefully parted the leaves. Yes! He could see the shape of two men scarcely twenty-five yards in front. He dropped back and expertly loaded his rifle, thanking whoever might be listening to his prayers that he was one of the few officers who could shoot as well as his men.

He knelt, bracing the gun against his shoulder. His powder and shot were ready, his ramrod to hand. He aimed and fired. The second ball, powder and ram were in the smoking barrel before the remaining man had time to turn. Seconds later Oliver fired and the rod of steel he had deliberately left in the barrel flew with horrific accuracy to embed itself in the chest of the second man. He died, a look of total stupefaction on his face.

The third man was on his feet, ready to run, but he was too late. Oliver crashed through the intervening bushes, his pistol loaded and cocked, his intention to kill written clearly on his face. The man threw down his weapon and desperately raised his hands. Oliver stopped and with cold deliberation pointed his pistol at the man's quaking chest. This was one of the evil vermin who had dared to harm his family. He would die, as the others had, for his temerity. Vaguely Oliver heard Peters and Murray approaching rapidly. He ignored them. With icy calm he began to squeeze the trigger. The man saw his death written on the captain's face and his bladder emptied.

'Captain Mayhew, sir, this man can tell us who sent him. He is more value to us alive than dead.' Peters spoke quietly from a position several yards behind the condemned man and his executioner. Oliver heard the words but for a moment their meaning eluded him. The man's life hung on a thread. Then the finger on the trigger gradually relaxed but the pistol was not lowered.

'Secure this man. I will interrogate him later.'

'Yes, sir.'

'And there are two more, bury them.'

'Yes, sir.'

Oliver waited until the wretched man, gibbering with relief, was tied before finally lowering his weapon. The red mist cleared from his vision and his bloodlust vanished. He was once more a man Sarah could have recognized.

'Is everyone safe, Peters?' He held his breath, waiting for the answer.

'I'm sorry. Captain, Tom is dead. He was too slow getting down from the box.'

'That is bad news. He was a good man.'

Then Oliver smiled and his tension drained away. 'Thank God! It is over. Sarah and Edward are no longer in danger. I just have to discover from that object who sent him and the job will be done.' He collected his discarded rifle and pushed the de-cocked pistol back into his belt before loping off towards the waiting coach.

Jenkins and Smith had dismounted and, abandoning their mounts, had managed to force their way through the close-packed sheep. Smith, a practical young man, had found a gate, opened it and was driving them vigorously back into the field.

Smith had discreetly covered Tom's corpse and Jenkins was at that moment assisting Sarah from the coach. She heard the crashing branches and stared into the green darkness unable to see who was approaching at such speed. Then her desperate gaze saw Oliver and her feet moved of their own volition and she was running towards him, her face alight with joy.

As he leapt over the small ditch he dropped his precious gun to receive her. She fell into his arms and he crushed her to him, unable for a moment to disguise his love. Sarah, who wept, her face buried in his shoulder, failed to see his expression but her son did.

Finally she was able to stop shaking, she drew back and scanned his face. 'I was so scared, Oliver. When I heard the shots I thought you had been killed.'

He grinned, his emotions back under control. 'No, my love. I am unscathed. But I am glad to say that two of your attackers are not.'

Edward had joined them and Oliver pulled him into the circle of their embrace. 'Did you kill them, Papa? With your gun?'

'Yes, son, I did.' The satisfaction in his voice made Sarah step back.

'You killed them?' She felt her breakfast about to make an embarrassing reappearance and she clapped her hand across her mouth and swallowed hard.

Oliver saw the dismay on Sarah's face and was angry. 'Of course I killed them. They were murderers, Sarah. What would you have me do, invite them to take tea?'

132

Sarah recoiled from the ferocity of his reply. She stared at the man whose arms had just enfolded her and saw a stranger. How could she be contemplating marriage to someone who killed without a qualm? Her eyes filled and she turned away from him, in that moment rejecting everything he stood for.

Edward, still clutching Oliver's hand, watched his mother walk away and knew his world was about to fall apart. He looked from one to the other, his face anguished. Oliver bent and swept him up in a bear hug. 'Do not worry, lad, your mother is overwrought. I will put things right when she is calmer.'

'But she looked at you in such a way, as though you were a stranger and she hated you.'

'No. It was shock. Your mother is a gently born lady; killing is not something she is familiar with. She does not fully understand what has happened this morning, nor why. I am a soldier, Edward. I am trained to do as I did.'

The little boy rubbed his face on his sleeve and gave a watery grin. 'I understand, Papa. You were doing your duty, protecting us. I think you are very brave.'

'Thank you. Now go and join your mother. I must organize our return to Rowley Court.'

Once the sheep were safely in the field and the lane was clear, Oliver was ready to lead his party back. This was not as simple as it might sound. Turning a coach and four in a narrow country lane was impossible, they would have to drive forward until a suitable turning place was found. Tom's body was another problem. Oliver decided that Smith would carry him back draped over his saddle. It could hardly be propped up inside with the ladies. His man left immediately; he did not want the occupants of the coach to have to see it again. They had already been distressed enough for one day.

Eventually the carriage was facing the correct way and Murray and Peters had completed their grisly task in the woods. Murray hopped onto the box, beside William, the under-groom, who was having difficulty managing the nervous horses on his own.

Inside, the women sat in subdued silence. Edward did not need to be reminded to sit still. Sarah was sifting her conflicting emotions and trying to decide how best to tell her family, and Oliver himself, that the wedding was cancelled. The engagement broken.

She twisted the engagement ring around her finger and wished she had never put it on. How could she have allowed herself to be trapped into such a misalliance? The threat to them was gone, so naturally the need for protection had vanished also. Everything had changed.

She would dismiss Captain Mayhew and send Edward to the young curate for his lessons. Her life could return to its normal peaceful cadence and she could put these past unpleasant weeks out of her mind. The decision made she began to relax opening her eyes to see how her companions fared.

Edward was staring at her, his eyes worried. 'It is a good thing that Papa was not hurt; he is the best father any boy could have, is he not, Mama?'

Sarah's heart plunged to her nether regions. How could she have forgotten Edward's feelings? It was, after all, the reason she had suggested the union in the first place. She forced her mouth into a poor resemblance of a smile.

'He is, my love. We are very lucky to have found someone so suitable.' Reassured, Edward flopped back onto the squabs and promptly fell asleep. The excitement and early start catching up with him.

Sarah had more than enough time to control her emotions on the return journey. As always she knew that practicalities must come before her personal wishes. Tom's funeral had to be arranged. He had no family; he had spent all his life at the Court. Her late husband, Jonathan, had inherited him with the estate.

Hepworth and Harriet would have to be informed; some-one would have to be sent to London to recall Mrs Thomas. She would not need her lawyers now. She had not changed her mind. She had, for the first time in Edward's seven years, told him an untruth. However much Edward loved Oliver, she now held him in such revulsion that even to keep her son's heart intact, she could not sacrifice herself.

She decided it would be sensible not to announce her *volte-face* today; she would get the funeral over with first. There was still a full six weeks before the date set for the wedding; plenty of time to inform her family and to send an announce-ment to *The Times*.

The staff had been alerted and were awaiting their return. Jenny Bates, acting as housekeeper in Mrs Thomas's absence, was standing grave-faced on the steps to greet them. 'I have put out a light repast; it is in the small dining-room, madam, if you should require it.'

The thought of food turned Sarah's stomach. 'Thank you, Jenny, but we are all too overwrought for food at the moment. Could you put something on a tray and have it sent up in a little while?'

Jenny bobbed a curtsy. 'Yes, madam.'

Sally guided a still sleepy Edward up the stairs and into his temporary accommodation in one of the rooms next to his mother's. Sarah dithered in the hall, uncertain what to do. Then Oliver strode up the steps and joined her.

'I sent Jenkins to Hepworth to inform them what has happened. I have asked Lord Hepworth to send a note to London requesting that Mrs Thomas and the luggage return forthwith.'

'I see.' Sarah's reply was frosty. 'You did not think it neces-sary to consult me first? Am I to have no say in the matter?'

Oliver was baffled by her reaction. 'But surely you do not wish to go to London now? Not after all that has transpired?'

'No, of course not, but I should have been consulted.'

'Sarah, I have too much to do right now to deal with your niceties.'

'I quite understand. In which case it might be better, as you are to be so much occupied, for you to remove to the Dower House. I would hate to interfere with your necessary duties.'

His expression hardened. 'I will remain here, Sarah. You cannot throw me from your door like a common thief. I am your fiancé and will be treated with the respect that is my due. Is that clear?'

Sarah quailed at his harshness. How could she ever have thought him a suitable husband? This man was hardly more than a ruffian!

'As you wish, Captain Mayhew. I will not be dining downstairs whilst you remain under this roof. Good day to you.'

She did not remain to hear his reply but retreated hastily up the stairs. She could feel his eyes boring into her back as she ascended and was relieved to reach her chambers unmolested.

Chapter Fourteen

OLIVER snorted in disgust and headed back to the estate office were his prisoner was being held. Time enough to smooth Sarah's ruffled sensibilities when his task was completed. Jenkins and Peters stood guard. The man, weasel-faced and stinking, had slowly been regaining his bravado. This ebbed away when his captor appeared in the door.

'Has he said anything?'

Jenkins shook his head. 'No, sir, not a word. I expect he is waiting to sing to you.'

Oliver twisted a chair and straddled it leaning casually on the back, a look of expectancy on his face. 'What is your name?'

'Davey, sir.'

'Excellent, we are progressing already. Who sent you?' Davey hesitated a little too long. Oliver's arm shot out and the prisoner felt his breath being squeezed from his throat. 'You are to answer immediately, do I make myself clear?' The softly spoken words held a chilling impact.

Oliver released his crushing grip and resumed his relaxed position, arms folded across the chair back. 'I will try again, who sent you?'

'Richard Fitzwilliam.'

The name sounded familiar. 'Why?'

'He found out that Edward 'averstock is heir to the estates wot 'e wos expecting to get so he gets us to kill 'im afore any other cove knows it.'

Oliver's smile did not reassure Davey. 'And where am I to discover this Richard Fitzwilliam?'

'I ain't got a notion; we never met the gent, a flash 'arry came to us at our crib wiv the instructions and blunt.' Observing Oliver's sceptical expression he babbled on. 'It wos by chance the flash cove let slip the name or else I'd not know that either.'

'Describe the man to me.'

'He wos tall and fin and wos wearing all black, and 'is face wos dark as well. I reckon as he wos about forty, or there abouts.'

Oliver was satisfied the man was telling the truth. 'Very well. Lock him up somewhere, Jenkins. Lord Hepworth can deal with him now. Come back here when you have disposed of him.'

Jenkins grabbed Davey's arm and pulled him roughly to his feet. Weapons were not necessary; the man was no longer a threat to anyone. He was led away terrified and broken. He almost envied his partners lying snugly in the soil, their troubles already over. His were just beginning.

Oliver yawned and stretched hugely. The interview had gone well, finally he had the information he wanted. The mystery was solved. He wondered how Sarah would react when he told her that her son was heir to an earldom.

Then his eyes narrowed and his expression hardened again. It was not over yet. He had dealt with the minions now he must deal with the paymaster. Although he recognized the name of Fitzwilliam he had no real idea where the family were located. Lord Hepworth might know; peers of the realm were not so plentiful that they did not at least recognize each other's names. Jenkins and Peters were returning. He stood up.

'Where have you stowed him?'

'In the wood store, Captain. We trussed him up like a fowl.

he won't be going anywhere.'

Jenkins grinned evilly. 'Apart from to the gibbet, that is.'

Oliver nodded. 'Good. I am afraid your work is not over. I might want you to travel post to London. If Lord Hepworth cannot help us you will have to find out what you can about the Fitzwilliam family and about Richard Fitzwilliam in particular.'

'I have heard that name before, Captain. Wasn't the colonel of the 15th Light a Fitzwilliam?'

Oliver banged the table. 'Of course! How stupid of me! Jack Fitzwilliam: he was a good man and he died a hero's death at Talevera. I wonder if it is the same family.' He stopped, lost in thought. 'Go to Horse Guards, I will give you a note. They should be able to tell us more.' He scowled. 'However well connected, Richard Fitzwilliam will pay for his plotting.'

'Topping an aristo is a hanging offence, Captain.'

Oliver's eyebrows shot up. 'Good God, man, I was not intending to murder him. No, I will force him to leave the country, exile him abroad.'

Jenkins grinned with relief. 'Do we wait for Lord Hepworth before we leave? If he knows about the bastard it will save us a load of trouble.'

'Obviously you wait. Jenkins, tell the others to stand down from full alerts but I want the regular patrols around the perimeter to continue for the present.'

Jenkins and Peters went about their duties and Oliver returned to the house. He could not expect their visitor for at least another hour, which gave him ample time to convey the astounding news to Sarah.

The only member of the household delighted by their return was Rags. He had regained a great deal of his old bounce and raced from room to room in an ecstasy of wagging. His exuberance cheered them, for Tom's death was weighing heavily on all their hearts.

After a brisk wash and change of clothes Sarah began to feel calmer. Had she overreacted? She needed to talk to Harriet urgently before taking an irrevocable decision. A tray with dainty bread-and-butter slices, cold cuts and tomatoes warm from the garden, had been placed, and ignored, on the side table in the sitting-room. Edward had fully recovered from his fright and was downstairs eagerly eating in the kitchen and sharing his experiences with anyone prepared to listen. Unlike his mother, his appetite was unimpaired by his adventure.

Sarah sat at her desk and tried to find appropriate words to tell her sister, Elspeth, and her dear papa that her marriage was cancelled. She did not, at first, hear the soft tap on the door. Obviously neither had Beth.

'Come in,' she called, knowing already that it could only be one person, insensitively invading her personal sanctum.

Oliver opened the door and stepped in, his expression watchful, unsure of his reception. 'I must apologize for disturbing you, Sarah, but it is imperative that we speak.' She opened her mouth to protest but he forestalled her. 'Not later, now. It will not wait.'

She sighed loudly. 'Oh, very well, you had better come in.'

He made no attempt to approach her, but remained just inside the closed door. 'I know why the attempts have been made on your life and by whom.'

Sarah sat up and her severe expression relaxed a little. 'The prisoner told you? Tell me, quickly.'

'It appears that Edward is heir to an earldom and vast estates and the heir presumptive, one Richard Fitzwilliam, wished to dispose of him before you discovered this for yourselves.'

Sarah's face blanched. Her son to be an earl? It could not be true? He was a little boy, her only child, how could he have connections elsewhere to people she had never heard of?

'Fitzwilliam? It must mean our name is Fitzwilliam, not

140

Haverstock. I can hardly take it in. Are you sure of this, Oliver?' In her agitation she had forgotten her resolve to distance herself.

'As sure as I can be without confirmation from London. Hepworth might know something of the family; you can ask him when he arrives later.'

'I am finding it difficult to grasp. If Edward is heir to an earl, will it change our lives?'

'I fear it might. If the present incumbent is old, Edward could well inherit before his majority.' He half smiled. 'I would say it is fortuitous that we are about to be married. The Earl is Edward's legal guardian and is entitled to demand that he makes his home with him. Once we are married this will not be possible.'

All vestige of colour vanished from Sarah's cheeks. She stared at Oliver in horror. This could not be happening, was she to be forced to marry him after all, or risk losing the most precious thing in her life?

Oliver mistook the pallor for fear that the unknown aristocrat would send for Edward before the knot was tied. 'We can bring forward the date, Sarah. The ceremony can take place three weeks from now, we do not have to wait if you do not wish to.'

'Why should this earl decide to send for Edward now? It could be weeks or even months before anything is heard from him.' She leant forward as a possible solution occurred to her. 'Indeed, if only Richard Fitzwilliam knew of Edward's existence maybe the earl will continue to remain in ignorance. I, for one, will not be contacting him.'

'Sarah, you have not thought this through. Richard Fitzwilliam will be forced to flee the country, or risk imprisonment or worse. Do you think his absence will go unnoticed?'

Sarah finally understood. She glared at Oliver. 'Fitzwilliam will have no need to flee if you do not force him to.'

'Good God, Sarah, the man tried to have you murdered. He cannot be allowed to get away with it.'

'It was my life and Edward's that were at risk, not yours. I do not wish him punished. I do not wish Edward to know about any of this. His inheritance is already more than enough. He has no need of a title or anyone else's monies. Why can that not be the end of it?'

He tried a different tack. 'It is not for you to accept or deny Edward's patrimony. He is a child now but will be an adult soon enough. It must be his choice, not yours.'

Sarah's eyes widened. 'I had not considered that. You are correct. It will be Edward's decision, but not now. My keeping him here with me will not prevent him from inheriting in the future. The title and estates will be there whether he is aware of it or not.'

Oliver's temper finally frayed. 'And what of the estates he owns? You would let them fall into disrepair and the tenants starve because you are too lost in your own selfish world to understand that responsibilities go hand-in-hand with privilege?' They glared at each other like a pair of scrapping cockerels in a pit, looking for a weakness they could exploit.

As they remained poised on the brink of further warfare his quick brain unravelled the subplot of Sarah's tirade. She had changed her mind. It was no longer her intention to marry him. They both knew that her opinions on the matter would be irrelevant if they were married.

Like Edward, in the aftermath of the ambush, he saw his dreams and hopes about to fall about his ears. The eventual acquisition of Sarah's money and estates, which had been his original reason for coming to Rowley, was now irrelevant. He loved Sarah and her son and losing them would destroy him. He blinked and forced his misery deep inside. He still had his pride; Sarah could never know how much her rejection had hurt him.

She watched the play of expressions on his face then saw

him turn his back and lean his head, for an instant, against the door. Then she saw him straighten, his head came up and he swung back to face her.

'I release you from your promise, Sarah. I have no wish to lock myself to an unwilling bride. The announcement will be sent to *The Times* tomorrow. I presume you will inform your family?'

There was nothing she could say. Her outburst, she belatedly realized, had revealed her intention. Oliver was behaving as a gentleman, allowing her to break the engagement without rancour.

'You have mistaken the matter, Oliver, I do not wish to release you from our engagement; I have not changed my mind.' Who was more astonished by her vehement denial it was impossible to say. Sarah had intended to accept his gracious offer but her mouth had shaped quite the opposite.

'In which case, Sarah, I will, of course, continue to honour your wishes.' He smiled warmly, all his former animosity gone. 'I will not search out Fitzwilliam, and be the one to bring his perfidy to light, if that is what you want.'

'Thank you, Oliver. I know the man deserves to be punished but I believe a higher authority than yours will do the job for us.'

'You must understand that the earl may still hear about Edward. Fitzwilliam had the information, so I think it is inevitable that in time it will filter through to him as well.'

Sarah was not to be discouraged. 'I, for one, am not going to worry about it. Time enough to take action when it happens.'

The sound of a carriage on the drive interrupted their *tête-à-tête*. 'It is Lord Hepworth. Shall we go down to greet him? I can hardly believe how much has happened to us since we saw him yesterday.' Her attempt to sound unmoved by what had passed failed dismally. Oliver stood aside, holding open the door for her to pass through, a pensive expression upon his face.

To Sarah's delight Lord Hepworth had brought his wife with him. She desperately needed the support and advice of another woman. Formalities dealt with, Sarah took Lady Hepworth's hand.

'I am so glad you have come, Harriet. Shall we leave the gentlemen to their conversation and retire to the small drawing-room?' Her voice sounded false and strained even to her ears.

Lord Hepworth fixed Oliver with a speculative stare. 'Something is not right between you two, lad. A blind man in a thunderstorm could see that for himself.'

Oliver dismissed Lord Hepworth's concerns. 'There was a problem but I believe it is over. I will tell you about it later. First, you have a murderer to deal with.'

As soon as the ladies were settled comfortably Sarah put the vital question to Harriet. 'Oliver killed two men yesterday and is proud of it. How would you feel if Hepworth did the same?'

'Proud to be his wife, of course. All men must be able to protect their families when the occasion demands.'

'But killing, Harriet? Taking another person's life?'

'Oliver is a soldier, Sarah, my dear. He must have killed dozens, maybe hundreds of men in the line of duty. Why should two more be a problem to you?'

Sarah thought for a moment, her friend was correct: part of her must have known that Oliver had a violent past, what soldier hadn't? However, the inescapable fact that she had agreed to marry a man with the blood from countless deaths on his hands had only truly registered when he had killed so calmly again that morning.

'It is ridiculous, is it not? To be so squeamish at this late stage.' Her face contorted with misery. 'Jonathan was so different; he had no violence in him. I do not believe I ever heard him raise his voice in anger, not even to a servant'

'I know I should not speak so of my son, but Jonathan was a weak man. He allowed you to rule him and that was not good for either of you. In Oliver you have found an equal. He is a far better match for you than my dear Jonathan was.'

Sarah's mouth dropped open. This had been a day for astonishing revelations. 'Jonathan weak?' she echoed faintly, too shocked to argue. 'Yes, I suppose he was. But I loved him, Harriet, and he loved me.'

'I am not disputing that, my love. I merely pointed out to you why you have made a better choice this time.' Harriet beamed. 'I have been far happier with Hepworth, you know.'

A maid came in carrying a tray of refreshments and conversation ceased until she exited again.

Sarah watched her friend busy herself with a chocolate drink and cut herself a slice of cake. 'Harriet, I do not wish to marry Oliver. He guessed my change of heart and offered to release me. For some inexplicable reason I refused and the engagement still stands. But he frightens me. How do I know he will not turn his violence on Edward, or myself, once we are married and are in his power?'

'Fustian, my girl, and you know it. I have never heard such Gothic nonsense! That is not the real reason you are having doubts is it?'

Sarah blushed, ashamed to be detected so easily in her prevarication, but refused to give an answer. 'Edward is the heir to an earldom, which is why someone wished him dead.' This announcement had the desired effect.

'Good heavens! That would, of course, explain it. Do you know to whom he is heir, Sarah?'

'We know the presumptive heir. The man who organized the attacks is one Richard Fitzwilliam. But the identity of the earl and the whereabouts of his estates is still unknown. We are hoping Hepworth might recognize the name.'

'It is a long time since he marched the corridors of power. He has not taken his seat in the Lords for years, but it is possible he will remember.'

'It would seem that I am a Fitzwilliam, not a Haverstock, which will take some getting used to.'

'I should not bother, my love. You will be a Mayhew in a few weeks time, after all.'

Sarah stiffened. 'I do not think I should marry Oliver, Harriet. He is not a suitable husband.'

Harriet chuckled. 'You are quite wrong: he will make you a very happy woman, if you give him the chance.' Sarah opened her mouth to protest but Harriet was in full flow. 'The sooner you are wed the better, in my opinion. This earl, whoever he might be, is now Edward's legal guardian and could claim him. Your marriage will put Edward out of his reach.'

Sarah jumped to her feet and began to pace the room in agitation. She stopped and faced her friend, eyes bright with indignation. 'So I must marry a man I do not care for in order to protect my son?'

Harriet was unmoved by this outburst. 'You will be doing no more than hundreds of others have done before you. And, my dear, you at least are not being forced to wed a man twice your age, as often happens to a debutante. Oliver is a handsome and intelligent man. He will make an excellent father and a devastating lover.'

Sarah's face went beacon-red; she was shocked to the core by her mother-in-law's frank speaking. By the time she had recovered sufficiently to answer, Harriet had smoothly changed the subject.

'Everything is in hand, my love. Your wedding gown is ready for a fitting. Shall I expect you tomorrow?'

'I can not contemplate such things until poor Tom is buried.'

'No, of course not, I apologize. I expect the captain will have it all arranged for Tom was well liked in the village; there will be a good turnout at the church. Hepworth will attend, naturally.' Harriet returned to the tray and poured Sarah a cup of steaming, aromatic chocolate and piled a pretty plate high with cake. 'Sit down, do, my dear, and have some refreshment. It will calm your nerves.'

Sarah subsided on the sofa and held out her hand for the cup. Harriet was right. She was doing no more than many women had been obliged to do. Oliver had not changed and neither had she. It was the circumstances that had altered. Sarah finally accepted that her main objection to the union was that matters had been removed from her hands. She was no longer in charge of her own destiny and she resented it, bitterly.

Chapter Fifteen

IMMEDIATELY following the coachman's modest funeral party, Oliver took himself off to London. He had decided, quite rightly, that if he was not there to quarrel with, Sarah was less likely to change her mind again and cancel the wedding.

Lady Hepworth thought his disappearance decidedly odd. 'Where did you say the captain had gone, Sarah?'

'To discover more about Richard Fitzwilliam and the earl.'

'I would have thought he could have sent one of his men to do that. His place is here, with you.'

'I am a little relieved that he has gone, for I am now able to walk around my own home without fear of confrontation or argument.' Sarah was forced to smile at her exaggeration. 'The only problem has been Edward's schooling. I have been obliged to send him to join the curate's small group at the Vicarage. Edward appears quite happy with the arrangement as he likes mixing with the other boys.'

The mantua-maker sighed. 'I'm sorry to ask, but please, madam, could you stand still for a moment or your hemline will be uneven?'

'I do apologize, Mrs Andrews. I promise to keep still until you have completed your work.' Lady Hepworth stepped back to admire Sarah's wedding gown. It was the final fitting. Once the hem was pinned, Mrs Andrews could finish the dress at her workshop in the nearby town of Market Camden.

'Yellow and gold was an inspired choice, my dear. The two colours perfectly complement your colouring,' Lady Hepworth said admiringly. The lemon-yellow silk underskirt fell straight from the high waist in shimmering folds. The gold sarcenet bodice and over dress with demi-train had no extra ruching or frills. The simple lines and lovely material were enough.

'The girls will look lovely in their dresses, Harriet. Yellow spotted dimity was also a perfect choice.' Sarah's lips curved in a small smile at the recollection of the pretty dresses her three flower-girls were to wear.

'There, madam, I have finished. Are you sure you would not like some beading, or tiny rosebuds around the neckline?'

Sarah shook her head vigorously. 'No, thank you, Mrs Andrews, definitely not. The gold lace edging on both the sleeves and sash are enough decoration.'

Two maids stepped forward and carefully lifted the dress over Sarah's head leaving her standing in her chemise and drawers. Harriet had abandoned any hope that Sarah could be persuaded to wear a corset and conform to the dictates of fashion.

'When you are dressed again, my love, shall we take a turn in the rose-garden before you leave? It is pleasant now the sun has hidden itself behind the clouds.'

Sarah's reply was muffled as she allowed herself to be reclothed in the smart, military style riding habit that she always wore. Respectable at last, her boots back on and the jaunty tri-corn perched on her head, she was ready to follow Lady Hepworth out into the rose garden.

Harriet was waiting, parasol in one hand, on the steps. 'I wish to show you the roses I intend to use in the house on your wedding day, Sarah. They will be at their peak by then, if we do not have another thunderstorm.'

Sarah glanced up at the sky. 'The clouds are too high for rain I think, at least for today.'

149

Twenty minutes later Sarah cantered back down the drive, Jack riding sedately behind. Late afternoons in July were not ideal for riding, they were too hot and humid, but she was still enjoying the freedom of being able to ride when and where she pleased after the restrictions of the past few weeks. Most of Oliver's extra men had been paid off and Rowley Court was peaceful and quiet, the way she preferred it to be.

To Sarah's dismay she arrived home to find a travelling carriage, drawn by two fine-matched bays, standing, apparently empty, on her drive. Her stomach plummeted as she dismounted. It could only mean one thing – the earl had sent for his heir and Oliver was not there to protect them.

Jack led her mount away and she hurried up the marble steps, habit clutched nervously in one hand, whip in the other. The front door swung open and Mrs Thomas waited to greet her.

'Two men have arrived, madam, they are from London and insist they will speak with you. I have put them in the small withdrawing-room to wait.'

'Where is Edward, Mrs Thomas?' In her panic she thought that her son might be spirited away that very minute.

'He is having his tea in the kitchen with Sally, madam. Do you wish me to fetch him?'

'No, I will speak to him later.' She hesitated, unsure whether to change before going to meet the visitors. She decided her need to know was more important than her appearance and walked briskly towards the small drawing-room.

A maid opened the door and she sailed in. From her calm demeanour it would have been impossible to discern her disquiet. Two black-garbed gentlemen were talking quietly, their backs to the door. Sarah found it difficult to swallow. A faint movement from her must have alerted them for they swung round to face her.

The smaller of the two beamed. 'My dear, Mrs Haverstock, pray forgive our intrusion but we felt that as you could not come to us we would come to you.'

The wave of relief that flooded Sarah almost overwhelmed her. These were her lawyers, the Messrs Digby and Digby.

'I am so glad to see you!' She paused to steady herself: 'It is so kind of you to make the journey all the way out here.'

'It is no trouble at all my dear Mrs Haverstock. It is our pleasure, we do assure you. We like to escape from the confines of the office, do we not, William?'

The taller, but otherwise identical gentleman, nodded. 'We have all the papers ready for you to sign, drawn up as you asked. It is very wise of you to protect your settlement.'

Sarah was presented with documents to sign and she did so without query. Robert and William collected all the papers, placed them in a box and prepared to leave. They had refused all offers of refreshment insisting that they had already bespoken a handsome dinner at the inn they were staying in overnight, at Market Camden.

Less than an hour after their arrival they were back in their carriage and bowling off down the drive. Sarah finally joined Beth in her bedchamber to remove her habit, its gold frogging and brass buttons no longer as pristine and shiny after her long ride.

'Will you be dressing for dinner tonight, madam?'

'No, I will dine in my sitting-room as usual.'

Beth frowned, it was overlong since her mistress had made the effort to dress and dine downstairs. Eating informally was comfortable in this heat but hardly fitting for a lady of Sarah's wealth and status. The sooner the captain returned the better. Mrs Haverstock would be obliged to dine downstairs then.

Sarah felt the aura of disapproval and knew the reason for it. She attempted to mollify her abigail with a glowing account of her wedding finery and the flower-girls' gowns.

151

'It sounds very pretty, madam, I'm sure. I wonder what the captain will be wearing?'

'I have not the slightest notion, Beth. I imagine his regimentals, although he has been absent long enough to have Weston make him an entire wardrobe.'

'Are you expecting him home soon, madam?'

Sarah smiled. 'I sincerely hope so; it is only three days to our nuptials.'

The door burst open and Edward raced into the room, his face wreathed in smiles. 'Papa is back, Mama. Jack saw him at the Dower House. Can we go and see him?'

'I think not, my love. It is too late to be gallivanting all over the park. Time enough tomorrow to bid him welcome.'

'Why is he not here with us, Mama? This is his home now, not the Dower House.'

That was a question Sarah would also have liked an answer to. 'It is customary for the bridegroom to reside elsewhere until the wedding, Edward. But I promise he will be here to see you first thing in the morning.' She hoped her answer would satisfy him.

'He has been away for so long; I have missed him dreadfully, and so has Rags.'

'And I have missed him too, Edward.' Sarah found, to her astonishment, that she actually meant what she had said. Without Oliver to spar with, life had been decidedly dull.

If Oliver was surprised by the enthusiasm with which both his betrothed and future son greeted him, he was too polite to show it. Edward flung himself into his arms.

'Papa, I have missed you so. Why did you stay away so long?'

Oliver picked him up. 'I must apologize, lad, I had much to do in town. But I am home now. Is Rags fully recovered?'

'Yes, he is as good as new.'

Oliver raised his eyes to meet Sarah's critical gaze. 'I have much to tell you, Sarah. My visit has not been unproductive.'

'Edward will be going to his lessons soon. You can give me your news when he has gone.'

'Papa, will you walk with me to the Vicarage?'

'Indeed, I will, Edward. Are you ready to leave?'

Sarah watched them go, Edward dancing along beside Oliver, chattering non-stop. Rags circled both, barking madly to attract their attention. They were so like father and son, they even shared the same floppy dark hair. Would it really be so bad to marry this man, after all they were almost a family already?

She had arranged to return to Hepworth House that afternoon to greet her family on their arrival. Her sister was attending alone, her husband felt himself above such things as a country wedding. Sarah wondered if his attitude would change when he realized that his nephew was heir to vast estates and an earldom.

Oliver returned and sought Sarah out in the study. Their greeting was awkward, neither quite knowing how their relationship stood. Sarah gestured for Oliver to be seated.

'It has been very quiet here without you.'

His mouth quirked. 'No one to argue with, my dear. There is nothing quite like a vigorous difference of opinion to liven one up, I always think.'

She spluttered, trying to swallow her giggles and suddenly all her reservations vanished. Oliver was once more the man she had chosen as a husband and father to her future children. 'I have missed you, Oliver. Especially yesterday: my lawyers came from London and I thought, at first, that they were from the earl, here to take Edward away.'

'Lawyers, Sarah? I thought you had decided not to see them?' His response was cool and he ignored her reference to the earl.

'The Digby brothers arrived here unannounced, Oliver. And I was so relieved they were not from the earl, I had not the energy to send them away.'

'What papers did you sign?'

Sarah's expression changed instantly from concern to horror. 'I have no idea, I did not read them!'

Oliver was shocked speechless by her admission. He stared at her, his expression incredulous. 'Good God, Sarah, how could you be so stupid? You could have agreed to anything. Where are the copies? You must read them immediately.'

'I have none. They took all the documents back to London.' She collapsed forward, placing her head in their hands. What had she been thinking of? He was right to name her stupid! Hot tears trickled through her fingers to drop unheeded into her lap.

'The sooner I take charge of your life, my love, the better,' Oliver murmured as he gathered her into the comfort of his arms. She relaxed and allowed his strength and heat to restore her. Gradually a different sort of warmth began to throb around her veins and she felt his arms tighten and his heart-beat quicken in response.

'Oh God, Sarah, you are so impossibly beautiful! Look at me, my love.' Sarah tipped back her head but she instantly recoiled from the passion she saw burning back at her. She was not ready for such a reaction. It frightened her. Nervously she tried to increase the distance between them, finding his proximity too disturbing.

Reluctantly Oliver let her move, knowing his vow to keep the union chaste was going to prove almost impossible. She was too damn desirable to resist. He held her captive at arm's length and grinned ruefully.

'I think I will rephrase that, my love: you are just plain impossible!'

Relieved he could joke about her rejection, Sarah returned his smile. 'I am sorry, Oliver, but I find I would prefer to wait until we are married.'

His rich chuckle filled the room. 'Good God, what sort of

man were you married to, Sarah? I was intending to kiss you, nothing more.'

She scrambled from the sofa and covered her annoyance by a flurry of dress moving and hair adjusting. When she felt sufficiently under control she answered. 'I was married to a kind and sensitive man who never once allowed his baser instincts to overcome him. He would not have dreamt of accosting me in such a way, downstairs, where we could be observed.'

Oliver finally understood. Passion was obviously an uncharted territory for Sarah. Her milk-sop of a husband had failed to arouse in her all but the most lukewarm feelings.

'In that case, my dear, in future I will endeavour to keep "my baser instincts" under control.'

She fixed him with a disapproving stare. 'I do not appreciate being found a figure of fun, Oliver.'

'Which is a great pity, sweetheart, as I find your behaviour a constant source of amusement.' Grinning widely he sauntered over and folded himself on to a convenient chair. 'Now, do you wish to hear my news, or not?'

'You are infuriating. If your information was not so important to me I would be tempted to box your ears.'

He leant forward, an answering gleam in his eyes. 'Would you indeed? That would be an interesting experiment! But, alas, one we will have to postpone.' His expression sobered and Sarah's heart turned over in dread.

'Is it bad news, Oliver?'

'Not really, Fitzwilliam is definitely your correct name. It appears Simon Fitzwilliam fell out with his father and went to live in India. He became a nabob and married an Indian princess.'

'I already knew all that apart from the name, of course.'

'Do you wish to hear the rest, or are you intending to interrupt continuously?'

Sarah smiled and waved for him to continue. 'It is through

him that Edward will inherit vast estates in Kent and the title. The present earl is two and eighty and believes that a distant relative, the Richard Fitzwilliam who has been attempting to murder you and Edward, is his legitimate heir. Richard's claim is through an uncle of the earl's.'

'It is odd that Edward's existence should go unremarked until two months ago.'

'I believe it could have been your advert for a tutor in *The Times* that led Richard to you. Until then they possibly thought that Simon's line had died out.'

Sarah frowned. 'But I advertised as Haverstock, not Fitzwilliam.'

'I imagine that Richard had already discovered the change of name. He has been living on his expectations for years and one can only suppose that he would wish to be certain that there were no barriers to his inheriting.'

'Did you discover his whereabouts?'

'Are you suggesting I broke my word, Sarah?' Oliver's demeanour changed and his expression was not friendly.

Hastily she reassured him. 'No, of course not. I am merely asking if your inquiries revealed where he is living.'

Mollified, he relaxed. 'Fitzwilliam and his family, strangely enough, are living abroad. His house in Surrey is shut up and his estates are being managed in his absence.'

'I am glad. If he is absent Edward and I are safe and the earl is less likely to learn about us.'

'I hope you are correct.' He stood, and offered her his hand, which she ignored. Her actions were noted. 'At what time will you be going to Hepworth, Sarah?'

'We are expected at three o'clock. I am glad you will now be able to meet my father before the ceremony.'

The happy couple and their son decided to ride over to Hepworth House. The need for either intimate contact or conversation was then eliminated. Lady Humphrey had arrived in good time and had been anxiously peering out of the window waiting for her younger sister's arrival.

'Sarah, you are in fine looks.' She reached down to pat Edward absently on the head for her full attention was fixed on the attractive man who had just dismounted athletically from his saddle.

Oliver strolled over and bowed, but did not attempt to take her hand. 'I am delighted to make your acquaintance, Lady Humphrey. Sarah and I thank you for taking the trouble to travel all this way.'

'Oh, Captain Mayhew, it was no trouble, nothing at all. Do you think I would miss my only sister's marriage?'

Sarah hid her smile behind her hand. Her sister was an inveterate flirt and was already trying her skills on Oliver. He was, she noted, apparently unmoved. 'Has father arrived yet, Elspeth? Oliver wishes to speak with him.'

Elspeth shook her head and her dark ringlets bobbed becomingly. 'Not yet, but he is expected at any moment.'

Edward had been ignored long enough. 'Will Grandpapa come and stay with us after the ceremony tomorrow, Mama?'

'I am not sure, my love. It is possible he will have to return straightaway; he cannot leave his parish unattended.'

All heads turned at the sound of wheels trundling down the drive. Sarah had sent her carriage to collect her father and it was this vehicle they expected to see.

Edward was the first to speak. 'That is not our carriage; look it has something painted on the door.'

Sarah was looking and her face paled. Her eyes flew to Oliver and he stepped over and he placed a comforting arm around her shoulders. 'Oliver, it is the earl come to take Edward away.'

Chapter Sixteen

ELSPETH, unaware of the significance of the crested carriage, trilled, 'Oh my, Lady Hepworth, you have a very illustrious visitor! Is it another member of the wedding party, Sarah?' Receiving no immediate response she glanced round and, becoming aware of the frozen tableau behind her, remained silent. For all her frivolity, she loved her sister and sensing something catastrophic was unfolding stepped closer to Sarah and Oliver, offering her support.

The smart equipage drew to a crisp halt. Two postilions jumped down; one let down the steps the other flung open the door with a flourish. Sarah, who was expecting an elderly aristocrat to descend, realized instantly that the three sombre-faced, dark-garbed men were lawyers. The constriction around her chest began to loosen – even three lawyers were preferable to one Earl of Westover.

Oliver's hand squeezed her shoulder and she looked up. He raised his eyebrow at the three men; Sarah nodded. He removed his arm and approached them, his expression no more than polite. He offered a cursory bow then waited for one of the trio to introduce themselves.

'We are here on behalf of the Lord Fitzwilliam, the Earl of Westover. We wish to speak to one Sarah Fitzwilliam.'

'I believe you are misdirected. This is Hepworth House. There is no one of that name residing here.'

The lawyer's eyes narrowed and he scanned the group at

the top of the steps. Sarah had pushed Edward behind her and it was impossible for the man to decide which of the three women was the one he sought.

Oliver remained alert and formidable, blocking their passage. The spokesman retreated and held a hurried conversation with his companions. 'We have already visited Rowley Court and were directed here.'

'I repeat, you have been misdirected and are intruding on a private party.' Oliver stepped forward and the men retreated further.

'We will wait at Rowley Court for Mrs Fitzwilliam's return.'

The coach door was closed, the steps removed and the postilions regained their places. Less than ten minutes after its arrival, the Earl's carriage left Hepworth House. It bowled past the vehicle carrying Sarah and Elspeth's father, the Reverend Peter Bartholomew.

The flurry of excitement caused by seeing her parent for the first time that year gave Sarah time to recover her equilibrium before the inevitable questions from her sister. Oliver, as expected, spoke formally to his future father-in-law, in private, and both emerged well pleased with the encounter.

An hour later, the family gathered in the drawing-room as Sarah explained the significance of the visit from the earl's lawyers. Elspeth was the first to break the stunned silence the revelation had caused.

'Edward is to be an earl and is heir to a vast fortune? What does he think about all this, Sarah?'

'I have not told him. I did not wish to worry him unnecessarily; he is not old enough to understand.'

'Quite right, my dear,' her father agreed. 'Time enough for explanations when he is safe.' His kindly, bewhiskered face, creased into a smile. 'I think you should be married immediately, Sarah, before you return home.'

Oliver stood up. 'I agree. As soon as we are married,

Edward will no longer be the earl's responsibility. I will be his legal guardian.'

'The banns have been read. You can be married here. I will conduct the service myself.'

Sarah stared at her father. 'Here? Now? Is that possible, Papa?'

'Yes my dear. I am an ordained priest and marriages can be conducted anywhere, if the banns have been read or a special license obtained.'

Lady Hepworth sprung into instant action. 'We are all here; it will be the work of minutes to organize things. It is fortuitous that Sarah's wedding dress is still here. Come, my love, you must get changed. I will call the girls.'

Sarah found herself bundled out of the room followed by Elspeth. She cast a despairing glance back at Oliver who grinned and shrugged. 'It is the only way, Sarah. I will return to the Dower House to change. I will be back within the hour.'

Less than an hour later Sarah was dressed in her wedding finery. Her nieces, Chloe, Charity and Lucinda, wore their matching dimity-gowns and even Elspeth, Sophia and Harriet had found time to don their best. Downstairs, Sarah's father waited, prayer book in hand, in a hastily decorated ballroom. Lady Hepworth's staff had worked miracles with vases of yellow, white and gold roses and elegant gilt chairs in rows.

Edward, having had everything explained to him, was somewhat subdued. He was also the only member of the small congregation unable to changes his clothes. His garments had been given a quick brush and his face and hands washed. Soon the excitement of the impromptu ceremony was enough to overcome his worry. His only regret was that Rags could not attend, for which everyone else was profoundly thankful.

*

Oliver, not in regimentals but a new broadcloth coat of sage green, close-fitting inexpressibles, a green and gold embroidered waistcoat and hastily polished Hessians, was the height of fashion. He also waited, checking his fob-watch every minute and glancing over his shoulder.

'Now, now, my dear fellow, do not look so anxious. Your bride will be with you shortly.' Sarah's father chuckled. 'You hop about like a man expecting to be jilted!'

'Things are not as they seem, sir. It is all such a damnable muddle!'

Reverend Bartholomew took Oliver's elbow. 'Come out on the terrace, my boy, and tell me what is troubling you.' The elderly vicar was so easy to talk to, so open and friendly, that Oliver found himself halfway through his story before he remembered he was talking to Sarah's father. It was far too late to retract. He faltered, but continued. 'So you see, sir, it was always my intention to marry Sarah, but never to fall in love with her. I find myself unwilling to shackle myself to someone who does not return my regard, but, as a man of honour, I cannot back out.'

Reverend Bartholomew regarded him with fatherly affection. 'Has my girl told you she does not love you?'

'She has made it plain that she originally selected me to fill her nursery and be a father to Edward.'

'And now?'

'And now she holds me in dislike – she was horrified when I dispatched two of her would-be assassins. I believe she is only marrying me to protect Edward from the earl.'

'I think you are mistaken, my boy. I have watched the way her eyes follow you about the room. Sarah has always been a stubborn girl but I am sure she will admit her feelings to you in time.'

'I sincerely hope you are correct, sir. It is too late to change course now for I can hear them coming.'

The Reverend took up his place in front of the two rows of

chairs and Oliver resumed his stand to the right of the aisle. He could hear the girls giggling in the passageway and then the door opened and Lord and Lady Hepworth, their eldest daughter Sophia and Edward and Elspeth walked in and took their seats.

The flower-girls began their stately progress down the centre of the ballroom scattering hastily plucked rose petals as they walked. Sarah had chosen to process alone as her father was no longer available to accompany her. She paused in the open doorway to collect herself. Slowly she raised her head, straightened her spine, and inadvertently her eyes flickered towards Oliver.

A handsome, fashionable stranger stood in his place. The casual, comfortable country clothes were gone. She felt herself colouring as her assessment was returned in full. Pale blue-grey eyes travelled from the golden yellow rose buds tucked into her hair down to her feet encased in dainty golden yellow slippers.

Oliver's mouth curved into a smile of such charm that for a moment she forgot to breathe. Light-headed, she floated down the room, swaying slightly, to join the man she had promised to marry.

In less than fifteen minutes Sarah was Mrs Oliver Mayhew. The ceremony was brief and the wedding breakfast would now have to be a wedding supper but Sarah could not help smiling. Oliver took this as an invitation to kiss his bride. Ignoring the assembled company he drew her into his arms. His kiss was gentle, no sign of the unnerving passion that had frightened her last time, and Sarah allowed herself to relax into the embrace.

Her lips softened under his and she pressed closer, feeling his heat through the thin cloth of her dress. Her fists, resting on the muscled hardness of his chest, slowly unclenched and slid around his neck. She loved the feeling of his thick, silky hair, beneath her questing fingers and she sighed with pleasure, allowing Oliver unfettered access to the hidden depths of her mouth. She shuddered and felt a sudden surge of unexpected heat flood her body.

He held her closer, angling his head to gain greater access to what was being so willingly offered. Sarah's father thought things had progressed quite far enough. 'Sarah, my child, let me offer my congratulations,' he interrupted loudly.

The words, spoken right beside her, caused them to freeze in embarrassment. Oliver realized his ardour would be plainly obvious in his skin-tight breeches and was transfixed with horror. It would be unthinkable to step away and reveal his predicament to the ladies.

Sarah, who had after all been married before, understood his dilemma. Skilfully she turned, keeping within the confines of his arms but remaining discreetly positioned at his front.

'Papa, I am so happy you conducted our service. I know it is not what we planned but it was still everything it should be. Thank you so much.' Her father stepped up and she presented her cheek for his salute. Next Edward flung himself into her arms, demanding to be kissed by both his parents.

Sarah moved away to be hugged by her sister, who whispered in her ear. 'I envy you, Sarah, your captain is a real man. You will be happy with him, I am certain of that.'

'I hope so, Elspeth. He loves Edward and that is all that really matters to me.'

Elspeth's look was incredulous. 'He loves you, you goose. If he did not I would have stopped the wedding.'

'What do you mean? Why would you have stopped the ceremony?'

'Remember you wrote to me asking for information about him? I discovered he was known to be on the hunt for a rich wife. But whatever his intentions at the beginning, he has married you for love, Sarah, not money.'

Elspeth released her sister who was instantly enclosed in

Harriet's plump arms. 'My love, I am so pleased for you both. You make the perfect couple.' Harriet clapped her hands. 'I have arranged for champagne and refreshments to be served in the dining-room, let us go in and toast the happy couple.'

Sarah felt Oliver thread her arm through his and with Edward hanging on to her other hand, she allowed herself to be guided from the ballroom, across the spacious marble-tiled hall, into the dining-room. Toasts were drunk and tasty food consumed allowing her no time to consider the import of Elspeth's revelations.

It was full dark before the newlyweds were waved off in the carriage used to bring the Reverend Bartholomew from his parish in rural Essex. Sarah sank back on the cushions and closed her eyes, not sure if the unaccustomed alcohol or confusion was making her head spin so alarmingly.

'I'm going to be sick.' Edward said and promptly was. Oliver, moving with impressive speed, was able to catch the mess in his hat. When Edward had finished retching, Oliver opened the door and tossed his new headgear, and its unpleasant contents, out into the night.

'Are you feeling quite well, now, Edward?'

'Yes, thank you, I am better. I think I ate too much cake.'

Oliver laughed as he wiped Edward's mouth with his handkerchief. 'Well, we can safely say that you no longer have any cake inside to upset you.'

Sarah was forced to smile. 'You are both quite revolting. I have no wish to discuss it further or I will be in need of another hat.'

The incident had not only occupied most of the journey but also stopped them worrying about what might await them at Rowley Court. Sarah had all but forgotten Elspeth's observations. Edward craned his head out of the window, which had, not unintentionally, been opened. 'The lamps are lit, but the drive is empty. The earl's coach is not there.'

164

'I should hardly think it would be; it is past ten o'clock,' Sarah replied.

Sally was summoned and Edward went willingly to bed. The late hour, combined with his bout of sickness, had exhausted him. This left Sarah and Oliver alone for the first time since their marriage.

'I am retiring now, Oliver. It has been a long and eventful day. Goodnight and thank you for your assistance.'

'Goodnight, Sarah. I am going to take a stroll round the garden before I turn in.' They nodded politely and parted, he to the garden and she to prepare herself for her wedding night.

Beth was waiting, all smiles and congratulations. She brushed out Sarah's hair to fall in a chocolate brown waterfall to her waist and then helped her into her delicate cotton lace nightdress. Sarah replied when obliged to but otherwise remained silent. Finally left in peace she was too restless and too nervous to climb into her bed. She went to the window and allowed the night air to cool her.

She knew her sister's assumptions to be partially correct for she had always understood Oliver's wish to marry money, but what about the other? She felt her pulse fluttering in excitement. If Elspeth was right then her husband was coming to her tonight as a man in love. His attentions would not be that of a man driven solely by lust.

She fanned her heated cheeks with her hands and turned to gaze across the room. She had never noticed that the marital bed was so huge. She could hear Oliver's returning footsteps on the terrace below, then the sound of the windows being closed behind him. She felt sick.

This union was her doing; she had selected Oliver to be her mate, to father her future children, but now the time was approaching for the consummation she was having second thoughts. All her doubts about his suitability and his blood-thirsty tendencies flooded back and she shivered, this time in fear. She was entirely in his power – he could use her as he wished. What if his inclinations were for rough handling?

Sarah realized she could not go through with it. She could not share her body with a man she did not love, even for the blessing of more children. She ran to the door and turned the key, then flew back into the dressing-room to lock the servants' door. Only then did she feel safe.

How long would it take her husband to mount the stairs? Would he rouse the house with his fury at being refused admittance? Sarah retreated to her bed which, now the doors were locked, seemed a refuge not a threat. She scrambled in and pulled the thin summer comforter up to her chin. She could hear her heart pounding in her ears and felt the cold trickle of perspiration between her shoulders.

Heavy footsteps approached her door. She froze, waiting for the handle to turn. The footsteps continued past the room without pause and vanished into the night. For a moment Sarah remained rigid, then slowly began to relax. Oliver had chosen to go to his own bed chamber. Perhaps he was more like Jonathan than she thought.

She snuggled down in the feather mattress and fell instantly asleep.

Chapter Seventeen

Oliver had been in the estate office discussing the possible introduction of Capability Brown's radical horticultural notions for at least two hours when Sarah appeared in the breakfast parlour. The usual covered chafing dishes filled with coddled eggs, fried ham and muffins failed to tempt her. Eventually she selected a slice of bread and butter and a single egg.

As she was toying with her meagre breakfast Oliver strode in. 'Good, I had hoped you would be here, Sarah. We have much to talk about.'

'About the earl and his lawyers?' she said faintly.

He turned with raised eyebrows from piling his plate with food. 'What else did you suppose I meant?'

Sarah frowned at the sharp tone but assumed the question was rhetorical. Oliver carried his breakfast over and placed it loudly on the white linen tablecloth. Sarah watched him pour himself a mug of porter, curious to know why he was so agitated. Settled at last, he spoke again.

'I sent Jack to collect the wedding licence from the vicar and take it to your father for him to sign.' He glanced up. 'It is essential that everything is legal or Lord Fitzwilliam might try and have it put aside.'

All Sarah's desire to discuss nocturnal visits, or the lack of them, vanished. 'You are Edward's guardian now; what Lord Fitzwilliam chooses to believe is not important. He can make demands but we do not have to listen.'

Oliver dug into his congealing breakfast with apparent relish obliging his wife to sip her tea whilst waiting for his answer. 'I agree that it is basically the truth. However, you realize that he is an old man and will wish to meet his new heir, sooner rather than later.'

'Immediately?'

'It is a possibility; an octogenarian has limited time at his disposal.'

Sarah's nostrils flared but she swallowed her annoyance. She smiled sweetly. 'I meant, do you think the lawyers who came yesterday will expect us to go back with them?'

He considered for a moment. 'It might be unwise to do so. He will be considerably put out that he was unable to snatch Edward before the wedding, if that was his intention. I will agree to a visit but not to accompany them on their return.'

'You will agree? Am I not to be consulted, Oliver?'

He seemed surprised by her query. 'Did you wish to be? Such matters are now my concern, but I will always discuss my decisions with you if that is what you would like.' He smiled, apparently pleased with his sensitivity.

Sarah lost her temper. She faced him, her eyes stormy and her cheeks stained with a hectic flush. 'How dare you talk to me as if I am stupid? I married you to run my estates and to be a father to Edward, not to interfere and order my life.'

'Do sit down, my dear, and please do not shout. I am not on the other side of the park.' His amused response was the fuel to her fury. Without a seconds hesitation she snatched up his half-eaten breakfast and tipped it over his head

She did not remain to gloat as the sticky yolk trickled down his face and the ham slid from his grease spattered hair onto his intricately folded cravat. She knew as soon as the food had left the plate that she had made a serious error of judgement. She had no intention of remaining in reach of his justified retribution.

She was at the breakfast parlour door when she heard his chair crash to the floor. Frantically she turned the knob but it was slippery under her palm and would not engage. She gripped harder and it turned. She had it half open when his arm slammed it shut again.

Her knees felt weak and her stomach churned. Before she had time to react further, Oliver's hands gripped her shoulders roughly and spun her around. His face was a mask of fury, his teeth barred, a feral glint in his eyes. Then she saw the tomato embedded in his forelock and, without thinking, she reached up to remove it. The unexpected gesture gave him pause.

'Oliver, you have got egg on the end of your nose,' Sarah said as though puzzled by its appearance.

'Sarah you are outrageous, absolutely impossible, what am I to do with you?' Oliver's mouth softened in a rueful smile and she could sense that his anger was subsiding. The painful grip on her shoulders slackened and, emboldened, she started removing the debris from his clothes.

'I am so very sorry, Oliver. I have quite ruined your neck-cloth.'

He grinned down at her lovely upturned face. 'Not to mention my dignity!'

Sarah giggled. 'Very well, I will not do so. You'll need to bend your knees, Oliver, if I am to remove the egg from your . . .' her voice faded as she saw something unwelcome flicker across his face.

He tightened his hold once more and inexorably drew her closer. 'It is strange you should mention my knees; I have just thought of a much better use for them.'

Sarah instantly took his meaning. 'Oliver, please, you cannot. I have apologized, please.' She struggled ineffectually but he was far too strong for her.

'Why should I not spank you soundly? Your childish prank deserves a suitable punishment.'

She struggled desperately, as her feet swung helplessly inches from the floor. 'You agreed you did not believe in physical chastisement.'

'We were, if I recall, discussing Edward, not a full-grown adult. I believe the situation to be quite different.' His tone was conversational, no hint of his former fury. Sarah finally realized that he was teasing. Her fear vanished.

'If you do not put me down, Oliver, I will scream. Edward is in the garden, do you wish him to hear me?'

Instead of releasing his grip he crushed her against him and plundered her open lips with a ferocious kiss that was more punishment than pleasure. When he eventually set her down, Sarah ostentatiously wiped her mouth with her hand, her expression wary. 'I think I would have preferred the beating.'

'Do not provoke me, my dear. My anger is on a very tight rein at the moment.'

'Then I will remove myself from your presence, Oliver, that way we can both be happy.' She reached the exit and had the door safely open before she continued. 'I think I just heard the sound of the carriage arriving. It might be advisable to change before you greet them.'

She heard a definite thud as a missile hit the hastily closed door then she gathered up her skirts and made a decidedly undignified retreat. When Oliver burst from the room he could hear her laughter still echoing down the passageway.

Unsure whether he was angry or amused but certain he was frustrated, he banged his fist into the wall before following Sarah down the passageway. He met Edward coming in from the garden.

'Papa, why do you have food all over your head?'

'A good question, son, for which I have no answer. Your mother is in the drawing-room, perhaps she can give you a satisfactory explanation. I, however, must go upstairs and change.'

'I came in to tell you that the men we saw yesterday have just arrived.'

'Thank you, Edward. Tell your mother I will join her directly.' Unwilling to be seen by anyone else wearing his breakfast, Oliver shot upstairs to his bachelor quarters. Jenkins, newly promoted to his personal servant, was wise enough not to comment on his master's appearance.

Freshly washed and clothed in another of his outfits from Weston, Oliver felt calm enough to speak. 'Jenkins have my gear moved to the master suite today.'

'Yes, Captain.' Oliver detected a distinct hesitation in the answer.

'And get Beth to move Mrs Mayhew's belongings to the adjoining room.' Oliver scowled. 'That is an order, Jenkins.'

'Yes, Captain. I'm sorry, excuse me for asking, sir, but does Mrs Mayhew know she is moving?'

'Damn it, Jenkins, what business is it of yours? Your job is to do as I tell you, nothing else. Is that understood?'

'Yes, sir!' Jenkins saluted smartly. The captain had the right of it. Neither he, nor Beth, need concern themselves with Mrs Mayhew's feelings in the matter. The captain was in charge now.

The visit of the Earl of Westover's men of business was brief. As the object of their journey had been removed from their jurisdiction all that was left to do was deliver the sealed and monogrammed letter and depart.

Sarah stepped forward, automatically holding out a hand, but to her chagrin she was ignored and the missive was handed to Oliver. She dropped her arm and pursed her lips, clamping back the exclamation of annoyance. She realized she would have to learn to live with being invisible, at least in public.

As the lawyers were being shown out Sarah tweaked the letter from Oliver's grasp. Before he could protest she had removed the wax seal and unfolded it. Quickly she perused the closely written content, keeping her shoulder between the letter and her husband. 'It is as we thought, Oliver.' She handed the paper to him. 'Lord Fitzwilliam wishes to meet Edward. He expects us to travel to Kent immediately.'

Oliver scanned the contents before answering. 'We cannot leave until the carriage returns from delivering your father home.' He thought for a moment. 'Are you agreeable to travelling to Westover at the end of next week?'

'If we must, then yes. Sally and Beth can go the day before with the luggage; they can take the old carriage. I suppose we will have to put up somewhere for the night. It is too far to travel in one day.'

'I will send Peters with the reply; he can also arrange our accommodation. There are several excellent coach houses on the Dover Road, any one of them will do.' He refolded the letter and slipped it into his pocket. 'If you will excuse me, my dear, I have business to attend to.'

'Are you dining in, this evening, Oliver?'

He paused at the door, obviously undecided. His mouth curved slightly. 'I will, if you promise me that my food will remain on the plate and not adorn my person.'

Sarah blushed. 'This morning's episode will never be repeated, I promise.'

'Until tonight, then.' Much to her disgust his smile sent tremors through her. She tugged the bell cord, hard. Mrs Thomas appeared a few minutes later.

'Mrs Thomas, Edward and I will be spending the day at Hepworth House. I would like the carriage outside in thirty minutes.'

Edward was delighted to be missing lessons for the second day. 'We will have to ride back, won't we, Mama? Grandpapa needs the carriage to go home in.'

'So that means you must change into your riding clothes and I into my habit. Will you tell Sally that you will be home at suppertime?'

Sarah spent a happy day exchanging news with her sister and father and the time for her departure arrived too soon. 'I wish you could both stay longer; it could be months before I see you again.'

'You and the Captain and Edward must come and visit us soon. Perhaps in October? It will not be so hot,' Elspeth said.

Sarah was unsurprised that this belated invitation was now issued. Sir John Humphrey would look quite differently on the heir to the Earl of Westover and, as his legal guardian, Oliver's status was immeasurably raised. Her reply was vague and noncommittal. Much as Sarah loved Elspeth half an hour in the company of her husband was overlong.

Reverend Bartholomew also issued an invitation but to this she also made half-hearted promises. The vicarage at Little Pickering was far too small and would necessitate a proximity to Oliver that she was not ready for. The ride back was accomplished without mishap, although Edward's pony had tried hard to unseat him when asked to break into a canter.

'Sally will be waiting for you in the nursery, Edward. You must have your supper there this evening.'

'Are you dining downstairs with Papa tonight?'

'I am and I have left myself too little time to change, so I must hurry.' Sarah stooped to kiss her son and they parted in the hall as Edward preferred to use the back stairs.

Her evening-gown was hanging ready and her undergarments were laid out on the bed. Her bath was a trifle cool but served its purpose. It had taken Beth some time when she first came to be in Sarah's employ to become accustomed to Sarah's unusual habit of daily bathing. The accepted practice amongst the gentry being to wash only their hands and faces and take a bath occasionally.

'I wish to have my hair in a loose arrangement, not in a coronet. It is too hot for braids.'

'Shall I thread silver ribbons through? There is a length that exactly matches your dress.'

'No, thank you, it takes too long. I do not wish to keep Captain Mayhew waiting tonight.'

'There's no chance of that, madam; he only returned himself a short while ago.'

Sarah felt some of the tension drain away. 'In that case, please put the ribbon in, Beth.'

Twenty minutes later Sarah stood admiring her reflection in the full-length mirror. She saw a stranger staring back at her. A slender, beautiful woman, with sparkling eyes and translucent skin. She compressed her lips to give them added colour then turned away satisfied she was looking her best.

Beth agreed with her. 'Madam, you look a picture! That evening-gown has never looked so well on you.' The maid stepped across, adjusted the heart-shaped neckline and puffed out the filmy silver gauze over-dress. Then she handed Sarah the ribbon that held her demi-train safely suspended whilst negotiating stairs.

Sarah floated down, head high, determined to behave as she should. She could not understand why, since Oliver's arrival, she had become little more than a hoyden. The problem was not Oliver's. She had known that he was arrogant and dictatorial when she had asked him to marry her. It was really she who should adjust her behaviour to accommodate him, not the other way round.

The drawing-room was empty. Relieved to be able to enter unobserved she decided to wait outside, on the terrace, for Oliver's arrival. The sweet scent of roses and honeysuckle hung heavily on the warm air. The sun, although lower in the sky, still shone with unabated warmth. Keeping country hours was, she decided, a disadvantage in the summer. How could anyone wish to eat an elaborate meal whilst it was still so hot?

Sarah thought she would suggest to Oliver that they dined

at eight o'clock in future, at least when the weather was so warm. She heard the drawing-room door open and close and turned to go in, pausing on the threshold to smile at her husband.

Oliver saw an ethereal vision clothed in silver and framed by golden light and his eyes widened and the blood pounded in his veins. Forgetting his vow to keep his distance until his wife reciprocated his feelings, he opened his arms and Sarah, to her surprise, walked straight in.

Previous animosity evaporated in the heat of their passion and for a few wonderful, heady moments, she allowed herself to be transported to another world. Then sanity reclaimed her and she drew back, her face flushed and her mouth swollen from his kisses.

'No more, Oliver. I am sorry, but I fear I am not ready for our relationship to become more intimate.'

With a wry smile Oliver released his hold and gently pushed a stray curl from her cheek. 'I am afraid my baser instincts overcame my self-control, my love. I can only apologize most humbly.'

Sarah smiled, unaware that her smile turned his insides over. 'It has been so long since I was a wife, I am afraid I am finding it much harder to adjust than I had expected. We scarcely know each other, after all. Two months is too short a time to become properly acquainted, do not you agree?'

'There is no need to explain further, my dear, I fully understand. I am content to leave things as they are until you feel more settled.'

'Thank you, Oliver. I gather you have moved your things into the adjoining rooms; that is sensible. It would have appeared odd if things had remained as they were.'

Oliver laughed, debating whether to tell Sarah he had attempted to usurp her room but been thwarted by her abigail and the housekeeper. 'Actually I had wanted to move into your room and transfer you to the adjoining chamber.'

Sarah laughed. 'I know, Beth told me. Poor Jenkins was thoroughly routed; it was unfair to send him on his own. He would have needed a regiment behind him to persuade Beth to give ground.'

'I am surprised that you have taken my presumption with such good humour, Sarah.'

'If you had succeeded I would not be so sanguine, I can assure you.'

Arm in arm and still laughing, they returned to the drawing-room to await the call for dinner. The meal was served *à la français*, and the dishes were positioned in the middle of the table, allowing them to help themselves. The first remove, which had included choices of succulent roasts and side-dishes, was cleared leaving Sarah and Oliver in possession of their plates.

Sarah peered over half a glass of claret. 'Cook has surpassed herself tonight. I am glad that I suggested the staff gather later to celebrate our union. There will be enough left over to feed everyone twice over. I have never known her present so many side-dishes.'

'Mmmm ... have you not, my love? I rather think the excess food is linked to your kind invitation to the staff.' Sarah put down her glass with such force the red liquid threatened to leap from it. Oliver prepared himself for an outburst but instead she laughed.

'That is ingenious, Oliver. I am glad they will share in such a magnificent repast. They deserve it. I will not feel so guilty when we send it back uneaten to the kitchen.'

He grinned as he refilled her glass. 'As long as you are not going to worry that you are eating the food from their mouths with every bite you take.'

'You are ridiculous, Oliver.'

Mrs Thomas and three maids came in carrying an impressive array of oval platters, which they placed efficiently in the space between them. Sarah surveyed them. 'I spy two kinds of fish, three pies and several vegetable dishes.'

'And I spy two pheasants, one chicken and three other un-identifiable puddings.'

'There is no danger anyone going hungry, I am delighted to say,' Sarah said shaking her head.

Eventually they admitted defeat and not caring to remain for nuts and sugared fruit they escaped the suffocating heat of the dining-room and retreated to the welcome cool of the terrace.

'It is pleasant sitting out here now the sun is set,' Sarah said as she spread out her skirts, ensuring her ankles were decently covered.

'I will send for a lamp in a little while, soon you will be invisible.'

'No, please do not, Oliver. The light will attract moths and I hate to see them burn on the glass.'

So, as the darkness fell, they sat companionably talking and planning, as married couples do. They retired to their respective rooms, both believing that their marriage was not going to be the disaster they had once feared.

Chapter Eighteen

'CAN Rags come, Mama? He will be very good and I'm sure that Lord Fitzwilliam will want to meet him.'

Sarah counted to ten before answering. 'I have already told you Edward, the journey to Kent is too long for a large dog to be shut up in a carriage. It would be extremely unkind to do so, you must see that.'

Edward stamped his foot. 'If Rags is not going then neither am I!'

Oliver strolled into the drawing-room, attracted by the shouting. 'Edward, apologize to your mother, at once, for your rudeness.'

The little boy took one look at his stepfather's face and hastily complied. 'I am sorry, Mama.' He hung his head and Sarah heard him sniff.

'That is quite all right, Edward. There is no need to be upset, I am not angry with you.'

'But I am, young man. I suggest you return to the school room and study your primer. I will inform you when you may come down.'

Thoroughly chastened, Edward slunk from the room without further dissent. Sarah waited until the door closed behind him before speaking. 'Oliver, I feel that was a trifle harsh. He is only seven, and he did apologize.'

'If I had shouted at my mother I would had been whipped. Being sent upstairs for such a misdemeanour is hardly a punishment at all, in my opinion.'

'Are you implying I am being too lax?'

'Yes, I am, but not irredeemably so, my love. He is a delightful child; he merely needs to know that he cannot always have his own way.'

'Oh dear, I suppose it is my fault. After Jonathan died he became even more precious to me and I must admit I find it hard to refuse him.'

Oliver grinned and folded himself on to a convenient Chesterfield. 'Obviously today you made an exception. I believe I heard him say he would not come to Westover with us?'

'He wishes to take his dog and I told him he may not.'

'I do not see why not? Having his pet to play with will keep him occupied.'

Sarah's mouth fell open. 'Oliver! Are you mad? The dog will drive us insane.'

'No my dear, he will not.' He was openly laughing at her. 'For I will not be in the carriage, I intend to ride.'

Sarah exploded. 'You wretch! It will be me refusing to come if that animal travels in my carriage.'

He raised his hand in surrender. 'I was teasing, my dear. If you do not to wish to take the dog he will stay behind. I can assure you Edward will not argue with me.'

Sarah looked thoughtful and her mouth curved into a mischievous smile. 'I have the perfect answer. If you are riding then Rags can run alongside with you. If he gets too fatigued then I will allow him inside for a rest.'

'I see I have no choice; you have me cleverly cornered. We will agree to share the treat. I have arranged for Peters to travel on the box with the coachman. Jack and Murray can act as postilions. Jenkins will ride alongside with me.'

'With only Beth and Edward inside it will be considerably more comfortable. Did the luggage leave this morning?'

'It did. I thought we should depart early and break for

refreshments at noon. Does that meet with your approval?'

Sarah nodded. 'Do you mean my kind of early or yours? Dawn or breakfast time?'

'Seven o'clock will be soon enough.'

The two-day journey passed uneventfully but all the travellers were relieved to see the imposing gates of Westover appear in front of them. Oliver reined in and waited for the carriage to pull up beside him. Edward, as usual, was hanging out of the window.

'Are we there, Papa? Are these the gates of Westover?'

'They are, Edward. We should be there in a little while.'

Sarah joined her son at the window. 'Can you see the house, Oliver?'

Oliver stood in his stirrups. 'No, the drive curves round and the trees obscure the view. But I can see the sea, Edward.' Edward lent so far out in his excitement that he almost pitched onto the road. 'Would you like to ride with me, son? Then you can see everything.'

With Edward perched securely on the pommel, Oliver urged Trojan forward. Sarah could hear her son exclaiming in delight at the vista presented to him. None of them had realized Lord Fitzwilliam's estates had the Channel coast for one of its boundaries. It would be Sarah's first experience of the seaside too.

Maybe this excursion would be more like a holiday than a penance. She smiled at Beth. 'It will be an experience to walk along a beach. I wonder what Rags will make of it?'

'He's a good swimmer, madam, so I expect he'll love it. Shall I tidy your hair and put on your bonnet, for we are almost there?'

The fetching chip-straw bonnet, liberally festooned with artificial cherries and tied with a matching ribbon, was replaced on Sarah's head. Beth smoothed out her mistress's cherry-red travelling dress and handed her her gloves.

'I hope that Lord Fitzwilliam is not a stickler for propriety, Beth. It is far too hot to be wearing gloves all the time.'

The carriage was travelling downhill and Sarah felt the coachman apply the brakes. Holding her bonnet, she peered out of the window. Her gasp was clearly audible even over the clatter of the horses hoofs and rattle of the wheels.

'My word! I had no idea!' She noticed Oliver had reined in again and was staring with equal astonishment.

It was Edward who broke the awed silence. 'It is like a palace, Papa. It must have at least a hundred rooms.' The sunlight glinted on the windows making the long grey-stone, crenellated building shimmer like a fairytale castle.

Oliver turned his head and understood Sarah's stupefaction. They had known that Edward was heir to a fortune but nothing had prepared them for the grandeur of Westover.

Sarah subsided onto the seat, her stomach agitated. Lord Fitzwilliam must be even more powerful than either of them had realized. She feared that even Oliver would not be able to stop him taking Edward away if that is what he wanted to do.

The nearer they got, the more impressive the house appeared. Their approach had been noticed and a bevy of liveried footmen awaited their arrival. An impressive, black-suited individual, obviously the butler, stepped forward to greet them.

'Captain and Mrs Mayhew and Master Edward Fitzwilliam, Lord Fitzwilliam wishes to welcome you to his home.' The man bowed and flicked his hand. The footmen flanking the long marble steps bowed in unison.

Oliver took Sarah's icy fingers and pulled them through his arm. Edward, subdued by the sheer size and opulence of his surroundings, hung onto his father's other hand. United,they followed the butler upstairs and through the opened double doors.

Inside, the walls soared to an ornate carved gallery reached by a pair of massive curved marble staircases. The housekeeper and an army of maids curtsied. The butler spoke, his deep voice sounding hollow. 'Mrs Mason will conduct you to your rooms. Lord Fitzwilliam will receive you in his private quarters in one hour.'

The accommodation allocated to them was equally as luxurious and spacious as the entrance hall. Sarah gazed round in awe. 'This room is as large as a ballroom! If I am obliged to leave my bed at night I am sure I will get lost crossing the floor.'

Oliver had chosen to follow her in instead of allowing Mrs Thomas to direct him to his own chamber. This breach of protocol had been accompanied by raised eyebrows and looks of scorn from the housekeeper, which they both ignored. 'This is not the main bedchamber. God knows how large that is! Shall we go and see?'

Edward was now enjoying the novelty. The astonishing fact that all this splendour and extravagance was to be his one day was quite beyond his comprehension, so he ignored it. 'Am I to sleep down here with you and Papa?'

'I expect you will be in the nursery, but no doubt when Sally finds us she will be able to tell you the arrangements.'

'I hope they have lots of toys upstairs.' He stopped and his face crumpled suddenly. 'I don't want to be on my own here. It is too big, Mama.'

Oliver knelt beside him. 'Then you shall not. There is room for a small army in that bed; your mother will not even notice you are there.'

Edward was too young to consider such an arrangement odd, but Sarah knew that Sally and Beth might wonder why she preferred to sleep with her son and not her new husband.

The door, hidden in the wooden panelling, opened into a similar, but even grander, master bedroom. They surveyed the acres of highly polished wooden floor, on which several large Persian carpets sat. The bed was so tall a flight of steps was supplied at the foot and so wide Oliver would be able to stretch from edge to edge with room to spare on either side.

'Can we all sleep in this room together, Mama? Then Papa won't be lonely on his own.'

'I snore so loudly, Edward, that I would keep you both awake. It is better for you both to sleep in a different room.' Oliver quirked an eyebrow at Sarah and she blushed but returned his smile.

Edward ran across the room to investigate the array of closets that faced them. 'Your clothes are in here Papa, but there is still room for hundreds more garments.'

Sarah could hear her abigail moving about next-door and was reminded that she needed to change. 'Come, Edward, we have little time before we are to meet Lord Fitzwilliam. We have to tidy ourselves. It is important that we make a favourable impression.'

When the summons came, all three were ready. Edward was the only member of the family eager to follow the footman sent to escort them. Sarah instinctively reached out and Oliver took her shaking hand in his. Whatever happened Sarah knew they were as one in their determination to protect Edward.

They were led downstairs and along numerous wide passageways until the footman halted. He rapped on a door and it was opened by a tall, thin man dressed entirely in black. 'Captain and Mrs Mayhew and Master Edward Fitzwilliam, my lord.'

An elderly man, impeccably attired in a navy superfine coat, elaborate cravat, plane buff waistcoat and knee breeches, greeted them with a beaming smile. 'Welcome, welcome, to Westover. I am so pleased you have come to visit me here. As you can see I am no longer able to travel far, or I would have come to Rowley Court myself.'

It was only then Sarah noticed that Lord Fitzwilliam was

leaning on two silver-topped sticks. She instantly decided that he was not fierce and autocratic after all, but merely an old gentleman eager to meet his heir. She curtsied gracefully and Edward and Oliver bowed. Oliver took her hand and led them forward.

'Captain Oliver Mayhew at your service, my lord. May I present my wife Sarah and son Edward to you?'

'Delighted to meet you Mrs Mayhew, Captain. Forgive my rudeness, but if I release my grip on my canes I will fall flat on my face.'

Edward giggled. He liked this benevolent old gentleman. He was funny. 'I am Edward and I am very pleased to meet you.' He walked up and gazed enquiringly into the earl's face. 'Can you walk with those, my lord? I expect it is very hard.'

Lord Fitzwilliam smiled. 'It is indeed, Edward, which is why I prefer to travel in my bath chair.' Expertly balanced on his sticks, he nodded towards a wicker contraption standing close by, which had two wheels to the rear and one in front. Edward was immediately fascinated and rushed over to investigate this strange vehicle.

'Look Papa, it is a chair with wheels, for adults to ride in.'

Oliver joined his son. 'It is indeed ingenious, son.' He placed his hand on Edward's shoulder and gently squeezed it. Edward looked up and recognized the warning there. Instantly he stepped back and bowed again.

'I am sorry, my lord. I am forgetting my manners.'

The earl's valet, a dark-visaged and strangely silent man, stepped forward and with the ease of long practice, guided his master to a high chair strongly reminiscent of a throne. Once seated it was impossible to tell that Lord Fitzwilliam was lame.

'Come and talk to me, Edward. I want to hear all about your life at Rowley Court. When do you reach your eighth birthday? Is it soon?'

Sarah and Oliver were ignored so they retreated to a sofa where they would not be overheard. 'I like him, Oliver. It is a shame he is infirm. He and Edward appear to be getting on. I am beginning to think that I have worried unduly over nothing.'

Oliver studied the old man and small boy, deep in conversation. 'I hope you are correct Sarah, but is too early to be certain. I must admit he appears friendly, but I will reserve judgement for the moment.'

'It's hard to believe Edward will one day, own all this. To run an estate of this size must be a difficult and time-consuming job.'

'I imagine it must be.' He paused, trying to phrase his next sentence in a way that would not upset Sarah. 'I think we will have to seriously consider allowing Edward to spend part of the year here, he will need to learn about his inheritance.'

'I realize that, but not yet, when he is older, perhaps twelve or thirteen, will be soon enough.' Pleased Sarah had accepted the inevitability, if not the timing, of Edward's departure, Oliver changed the subject.

Two days passed in a whirl of activity aimed solely at pleasing Edward. They all especially enjoyed the trips to the beach. They had been warned not to venture out onto the flat sands when the tide was rising, because it came in so fast it would be easy to be cut off and drown. Edward had seen a large wreck on the beach and was determined, before the visit ended, he would get out to explore it, in spite of the warnings about the tide.

On the third day, Oliver and Sarah were strolling together on the manicured lawn. To the uninitiated observer they were a perfect, happy couple. 'Now that you and Edward are settled here I intend going to London for a few days to visit our lawyers. I would like to read those papers you signed, if you have no objection, Sarah?'

She shook her head. 'No, of course not. I am sure there is nothing sinister in the fact that Mr Digby took them back to town with him. When are you planning to leave?'

'Before breakfast tomorrow. At least when I am gone you will not have to endure the ridiculous rigmarole at dinner-time.'

'Thank heavens for that! The food is appalling, quite cold and so much of it! And all the scraping and unnecessary bowing that accompanies it! I do not suppose it will be any more palatable when it is served on a tray in my rooms but at least I can leave it without being made to feel ungrateful.'

'I wonder if Lord Fitzwilliam fares any better in his chambers? Perhaps at his advanced age, food is of no importance to him.'

'There is one thing I would like you to do Oliver, before you depart tomorrow. Could you speak very firmly to Edward about the danger of going down to the beach unaccompanied? I fear he is determined to slip away with Jack and investigate the wreck on the sands.'

'I will speak to both of them. They will be left in no doubt what will happen if they dare to disobey.'

Sarah laid a hand on his arm. 'I think this is the one and only time that I can agree that you may use the threat of corporal punishment. It is better to be scared of being beaten than for Edward to risk his life.'

'Are you quite sure about this, Sarah? You understand that if he disobeys, I will be obliged to carry out my threat?'

'There will be no need to do that. Edward might sometimes consider ignoring my instructions but he would never disobey you.'

Oliver left Westover at dawn with the intention of staying in Town for several days. He had omitted to tell Sarah that he was hoping to continue his investigations into the assassination attempts. He believed that he was released from his earlier promise to Sarah not to follow up the information about Richard Fitzwilliam, now that there was no longer the need to keep Lord Fitzwilliam in ignorance of Edward's existence.

Chapter Nineteen

'WHY can't we go and explore the wreck, Mama? The tide is so far are out you can't see the sea any more.'

'Remember what Lord Fitzwilliam and Papa told you, Edward. The water comes in so fast you could not out-run it if you were caught out there. I am sorry but the answer must be no. Shall we go for a ride instead?'

Edward stared morosely at the distant wreck. 'Will Papa take me when he comes back from town?'

'You will have to ask him, Edward. It is possible. Now, are we going to ride or not?'

'Ride. Can Jack come with us?'

Sarah was relieved that she had persuaded her son not to venture out onto the sands to investigate the sunken ship. The fact that it was totally submerged at high tide, made it all the more alluring to a small inquisitive boy.

The next few days slipped by. Edward spent an hour or so each morning talking to Lord Fitzwilliam and being instructed on his future duties. The army of indoor and outdoor servants catered to their every whim and now that she was free to take her meals with Edward in the privacy of her sitting-room Sarah was beginning to enjoy her enforced stay. To her surprise she was missing Oliver and was almost counting the hours to his return.

On the fifth day following her husband's departure, Sarah

and Edward took up what had become their usual place on the terrace. It was here that Edward studied his lessons and recited his Latin verbs overseen by his mother. The school rooms at Westover were too hot and stuffy for comfortable learning whilst the weather was so warm.

Sarah handed Edward his slate and they were ready to begin. Rags was flopped on the flagstones enjoying the shade. He had discovered that a warren of unsuspecting rabbits occupied the dunes above the beach and spent most of his time endeavouring to catch them and, when that failed, trying to dig them out of their holes.

'Shall I copy out the sentences I studied last night?'

Sarah was about to answer when a faint noise from above made her glance upwards. Her eyes widened as she watched one of the enormous carved pottery urns that decorated the balconies begin to rock.

She screamed a warning and, diving forward, took Edward with her in a flurry of skirts. The falling masonry rained down on her back but her body protected Edward from injury. She lay rigid with fear, anticipating a crushing weight that would put paid to her existence and praying desperately that whatever the outcome her son would be unharmed.

The explosion of pottery and stones took place three feet to the right of her sending further debris flying into the choking dust that surrounded the prostrate figures. Coughing and spluttering, but miraculously uninjured, Sarah and Edward pulled themselves up to a sitting position to gaze about in amazement at the chaos that surrounded them.

'Are you hurt anywhere, Edward?'

Edward rubbed a dirty hand across his face. 'You squashed all my breath out Mama but I am recovered now.' Then his grin changed to concern. 'You are bleeding. There is blood all over your back and your dress is torn.'

Only then did Sarah become aware of the pain of the dozens of small lacerations caused by the falling stones. She winced as she moved her shoulders. 'I am sure it is nothing serious, my love. I have a few small cuts, that is all. When we go in Beth will be able to clean them up for me.'

Edward then remembered his pet. Had his dog been injured too? He scrambled up, scattering stones and dust, to look where his dog had been lying. The space was empty. 'Rags is unhurt. But where is he, Mama? Do you think he has run away because he was scared?'

Sarah was concerned that the accident appeared not to have attracted any attention. Surely, even in such a vast establishment, someone must have seen what happened? Why was no one coming to their assistance?

Then she heard Edward's dog barking angrily and raised voices from inside. She was starting to feel rather weak and knew she needed assistance if she was not to frighten Edward again by swooning right away.

'Call Rags, darling, he is stopping someone from coming out to help us.'

Edward shouted for his dog and Rags backed out of the open terrace doors leading to the library, still growling and with his hackles up. Symonds, the earl's manservant, emerged, his face pale, followed by two anxious parlourmaids and a footman.

'Mrs Mayhew, I have sent for your own girl to help you and also for the doctor. I cannot understand how such a thing could have happened. It is a miracle you were not both seriously hurt.'

Edward grabbed the rope looped round his dog's neck. 'Be quiet boy. Mr Symonds has come to help us. Bad dog, you must not growl at him.'

Sarah had managed to pull herself upright and was leaning precariously against the wall. She was unable to answer. Her horrified gaze was riveted to the smashed remains of the huge pot. The chair and table upon which Edward had moments before been sitting were invisible under the rubble.

If she had not looked up and been given those precious seconds to knock him out of danger he would be lying dead, his body crushed under the wicked shards.

She closed her eyes and thanked God for answering her prayers. Her own injuries were of no importance compared to Edward's safety.

'Mama, are you going to swoon? You have gone very white.' His tentative enquiry recalled Sarah to her surroundings and her eyes refocused.

'No, Edward, I was feeling a trifle giddy but I am almost recovered now.'

Symonds and the servants remained at a distance, unable to approach as the dog leapt forward every time he attempted to do so. 'Your girl is here, madam, and the housekeeper, they will be able to assist you to your chambers.'

'Oh madam, what a dreadful thing to happen! Let me put this wrap around your poor back then Mrs Mason and I will help you to your room.'

Sarah gritted her teeth and allowed Beth to take one elbow. With slow, painful steps, Sarah managed to negotiate the endless corridors and marble stairway and eventually reached the security of her room.

Edward, Rags held firmly in one hand, hovered behind his mother. He knew his dog was not permitted inside but, in the circumstances, nobody protested. Sally met him outside their suite of rooms.

'Edward, that dog is not allowed up here. Madam would not wish you to get into trouble. Shall we take him back to the stables? Jack will take care of him for you.'

The door had been firmly closed behind his mother; he was obviously not wanted in there.

'Rags tried to bite Mr Symonds. That's why I am holding on to him so tightly. It is not like him to behave in such a way.'

'One more reason to get him out of here.' Sally decided to take them down the back stairs. She, like all the indoor staff, was terrified of the autocratic butler and it was he that had banned the dog.

Edward ran ahead with Rags bounding along beside him, showing no further inclination to attack anyone. William the coachman and Billy were busy grooming two of the carriage horses but they paused as he ran in.

'Where is Jack, Billy? He must take Rags: he tried to bite Mr Symonds after the big pot almost fell on us.'

'Whoa, youngster, slow down a bit. What pot are you talking about?' William said, grinning as he put down his currycomb. Peters appeared in the tack-room door. He was not smiling.

'Tell me what happened, Master Edward. All of it, nice and slow now.'

Edward's anxiety about his mother returned as he saw Peters's serious expression. 'We were sitting on the terrace when a huge, enormous pot thing fell off the balcony. If Mama had not pushed me out of the way it would have landed right on top of me.'

This news was received in silence. All three men exchanged worried glances. Peters spoke first. 'Was Mrs Mayhew hurt in any way, Master Edward?'

Edward nodded, tears welling, as he remembered the blood trickling down his mother's back. 'Some stones fell on her and have cut her back and shoulders. But she was able to walk upstairs with only Beth to help her.'

'Has the doctor been sent for, do you know, Master Edward?'

'Yes, Mr Symonds said he had done so.'

Jack walked through the arch, leading Edward's grey pony. 'What is all the excitement about? There's a big fuss going on up the house.'

Edward ran to Jack. 'A big pot thing fell off the balcony and Mama has been cut a little. And you must keep Rags away from the house because he tried to bite Mr Symonds.'

Jack automatically took hold of the dog's rope-collar. 'Whatever next? Rags is a gentle animal. Why ever has he taken against Mr Symonds, I wonder?'

No one was prepared to answer, not with Edward there, but the tension in the stable yard was palpable. Peters turned to Jack. 'I will go up to the house and see what's what. You take the lad and the dog down to the beach for a bit.' Peters waited until Edward had disappeared before continuing. 'I think the captain should be sent for. I'll take a quick look round and then go up to town myself. Will you saddle up the big bay gelding, King John, William? I will be ready to leave in an hour.'

In the bedchamber Sarah was prone on the bed whilst Beth gently swabbed the scratches and cuts.

'Are they bad, Beth? Will they need sutures?'

'No, madam, I think not. One or two are quite nasty, but most are little more than grazes.'

'They are sore, I know that much. But we were so lucky. Had I not looked up when I did, God knows what would have happened.'

'It's a scandal, madam. They think they are so grand here but they can't even take care of their balconies. If the urn was so dangerous it should have been removed, not left there to fall on an unsuspecting body.'

'It is probably because it is such a vast establishment, Beth, that things can get overlooked. It was a dreadful accident but luckily we were not seriously hurt. I am more concerned about Rags. If he has turned vicious I cannot allow Edward to keep him.'

'That dog is the softest animal alive, madam; he would not hurt a fly – unless they tried to harm Master Edward, of course!'

'Rags must be kept at the stables in future and not allowed to roam loose until Captain Mayhew returns and decides what to do with him.' Sarah flinched as a piece of grit was removed. 'How much longer will you be, Beth?'

'I have almost done, ma'am. There – finished. I don't think I need to put on a dressing. Now it's all cleaned up its not half as bad as I thought.'

'I must get dressed again immediately. Do I have a loose, high-necked gown that will cover my injuries?'

Sarah rolled carefully off the bed and stood upright. Her back stung and it was painful when she moved her shoulders but she believed her injuries would be no more than a minor inconvenience. She could hear her maid rummaging through the gowns in the dressing-room and was grateful that it was warm enough to be left waiting in her undergarments without the danger of taking a chill. She wished Oliver had returned. The accident had made her nervous and brought all the old anxiety flooding back.

London was comparatively quiet. The season was over and the *ton* had departed to their various rural retreats. However, Parliament was still in session so Whites and Boodles were busy. Oliver, a member of both since obtaining his majority, walked briskly down St James's Street. He decided to try Whites first.

His session with Digby and Digby had been satisfactory. The papers Sarah had signed were exactly what she had asked for. They secured her own settlement and made sure that Edward's portion was inviolate. He had been interested to note that Sarah had made provision for any future children she might have.

The meetings with the Fitzwilliam lawyers had also been successful. When Edward eventually inherited Westover the transfer of power to himself would be smooth. As the future Lord Fitzwilliam's legal guardian, the running of the estate and control of the fortune involved would automatically be reassigned to him. He smiled ruefully as he marched along the busy street. He had decided to find himself a rich widow to marry but never imagined he would be given so much responsibility and power. He would give it all up in an instant if by so doing he could win Sarah's love.

Whites, at four in the afternoon, was relatively quiet but Oliver hoped the man he sought was in there somewhere. He greeted a few acquaintances, thanking them politely for their congratulations on his marriage, but continued to thread his way through the overstuffed leather chairs and side-tables.

If on the premises, his quarry must be in one of the side rooms, probably dipping deep as usual. The panelled room he entered was thick with wine fumes and perspiration. The four men sitting round the central table had obviously been playing cards all day.

Oliver hesitated – this was probably not an auspicious time to interrupt a quartet of hard-drinking gamblers. The youngest of the men, of medium build, his gingery hair cut short *à la Brutus*, glanced up, his expression irritated. He did not like to be disturbed when gaming.

'Good God! Mayhew! Where did you spring from?' Lord Henry Gibbons, 27th Earl of Enford, dropped his cards and pushed his chair back. 'I am out. My stake is forfeit. I bid you good day gentleman.' Henry Gibbons, whose life Oliver had saved twice when they were serving together on the Peninsula, joined him at the door pausing only to snatch up his mangled neck-cloth and jacket from a table-top, as he passed.

'It is good to see you again, my friend.' Henry flung his arm around Oliver's shoulders. 'I hear felicitations are in order? The word is you have landed firmly on your feet and caught a wealthy young widow in your net.' He felt Oliver's muscles bunch under his loose hold and dropped his arm. 'Did I get it wrong, old fellow? Have I offended you?'

Oliver relaxed and grinned. 'Yes and no, Harry. Yes, I have married a beautiful, spirited, adorable young widow and no,

195

I do not care a fig for the money.' His grin became even wider. 'I never thought I would ever be able to say this, but I am neck and crop in love with my wife. It is the reason I married her and whatever you might have heard to the contrary is incorrect.'

'My God! Struck down by Cupid in your prime! Well done, Oliver. I sincerely envy you. Am I to get an invitation to meet this paragon of beauty?'

'Anything is possible, but I do not think my wife is quite ready for you. She has led a sheltered life.'

The two men found an empty room and went in, closing the door firmly behind them. Oliver got straight to the point. 'I need some information, Harry, about a Richard Fitzwilliam. He has an estate in Hertfordshire and as that is your home too, I am hoping you can tell me something about him.'

'Richard Fitzwilliam, yes, I do know him. His estates run parallel to mine. He is not precisely a friend, but definitely an acquaintance. What do you wish to know?'

'His financial circumstances, family, anything and everything. I will explain why I need this information later.'

'Richard is one of the warmest men in England. He inherited millions from his maternal grandfather. He is pleasant enough. He and his family spend half their life aboard a yacht he had commissioned for him. He is married and has offspring, but I have no recollection of their ages or sex.'

'Is he abroad now?'

'Actually I think I heard he has returned prematurely; his mother has been taken ill, I believe. He has been back in residence for a few weeks at that monstrosity he had built for himself. I have never visited, but I understand it rivals The Pavilion for vulgarity and size.'

Oliver rubbed his eyes, his thoughts troubled. 'I will explain why I need to know.' When he had finished his tale Henry shook his head.

'You have the wrong cat up your tree, Oliver. Fitzwilliam

196

has no interest in the title; he is something of a Republican in his sympathies. Now, if you had been accusing him of being a Bonapartist and aiding the enemy, I might have been interested.'

'Then who in God's name has been trying to harm Edward and Sarah? The man I captured named Fitzwilliam and he was too terrified to lie to me, I can assure you.' Oliver frowned and sought back over exactly what his prisoner had said. Something was niggling at the fringes of his memory. 'God's teeth! I have it now!' He slammed his hands on the table with such force Henry recoiled. 'The prisoner described the go-between as dark-visaged, black-garbed and well spoken. I have actually encountered a man who meets that description but failed to realize it. I have been searching in the wrong direction all this time.'

'Explain yourself Oliver. Who is the murdering bastard, if it is not Fitzwilliam?'

'Westover is behind the attacks. His manservant, Symonds, is the go-between.'

'Are you certain?' Henry sounded as horrified as he looked.

'Yes, it makes perfect sense.'

'For God's sake man, why are you still sitting here? Your wife and stepson are in Westover's power. With you absent he has free rein to attack again!'

The blood drained from Oliver's face. He should not have needed his friend to point this out to him but for a moment his brain had refused to recognize the importance of his discovery. It was too awful to contemplate. He had blithely ridden off leaving his beloved wife at the mercy of a ruthless killer. Finally his limbs responded to his will. He was on his feet and out of the door before Henry could wish him 'God speed!'

Chapter Twenty

'THERE is a basket of fruit for you, madam,' Beth said, staggering across Sarah's private sitting-room.

'Good heavens! We will never eat all this. The three vases of flowers that have already arrived are sufficient apology. I wonder what will be sent up next?'

Edward was already investigating the basket. 'May I have a peach, Mama?'

'Yes, darling, of course. Do you wish to finish this game or shall we consider it a draw?'

Edward, chin dripping with peach juice, grinned. 'I was winning, you know I was.'

'Very well, I admit defeat.' She handed him a napkin. 'Go and sit down and eat that, please, it is dripping on the carpet.' She watched him curl up in the window seat, glad he was, for the moment, content to remain indoors with her. There was a knock at the door. Beth hurried over to answer it and was informed by a footman that the doctor had arrived. 'Dr Radcliff is here, madam. Do you still wish to see him?'

Sarah considered. 'Yes, I suppose I must. It would be discourteous to send him away without a least speaking to him. Ask him to come up.' Beth relayed the message and closed the door.

Sally took Edward's hand. 'Come along Master Edward, we will go upstairs. Madam is having a visitor.'

Edward was happy to go after Sarah gave him permission

to select two more pieces of hothouse fruit to take up to the nursery with him.

Dr Radcliff was short and stout, his black waistcoat buttons straining. 'My dear Mrs Mayhew, what a dreadful experience for you. I have come at once to attend you. Lord Fitzwilliam is a dear and valued patient and has asked me to take especial care of you.' The doctor dropped his medical bag on the floor and bowed politely.

Sarah nodded, she was too sore to do more. 'Thank you for attending so promptly, Dr Radcliff. However, I am pleased to say that your visit is unnecessary. My injuries are minor and my maid has dealt with them.'

The doctor beamed. 'Excellent, Mrs Mayhew. I am delighted that you do not need my services. But if you feel feverish or unwell in any way please do not hesitate to send for me at once.'

Sarah offered her hand. They exchanged farewells and the doctor departed. 'It was kind of Lord Fitzwilliam to engage his own physician, wasn't it, madam?'

'It was, Beth, but I would expect no less. For he has shown us nothing but friendliness and courtesy since we arrived. It is hardly his fault an urn fell from the balcony.' She walked slowly over to the window. The midday sun glinted on the sea. 'It is almost high tide. There is so much water – it appears to fill the horizon.' She smiled. 'It is easy to see why the ancients believed the world was flat. If I did not know better I would think so myself.'

Beth joined her at the window. 'I don't like the way the sea rushes in so fast, madam. I watched it yesterday. One minute that old wreck was there and the next it was swallowed by the racing water. It fair scared me, it did. I'll be glad to get back to the country: you know where you are with trees and such.'

Sarah laughed. 'We will be returning in a week or so, I promise. Lord Fitzwilliam wishes Captain Mayhew to spend some time inspecting the estate with his manager. But after that we will be free to return to Rowley Court.' She attempted to sit in a high-back chair but found it too uncomfortable. Restless, Sarah got up and walked around the room. 'Beth, will you send for Jack. I must speak to him.'

She perched on the window-seat and waited. When Jack arrived he was uneasy and not his usual cheerful self. Sarah got straight to the point. 'Jack, I am concerned that Rags has been altered in some way by his poisoning. I wish you to keep him restrained at all times. Edward must only see him when you are there, is that clear?'

Jack shifted uncomfortably and mumbled. 'Yes, ma'am, I understand.'

'What is wrong, Jack? Is there something you are not telling me?'

Miserably, Jack looked up. 'I'm sorry ma'am, but the dog's run off. I took him back, like you told me, and tied him up in the stable yard, but somehow he got free. I've been searching for him this past hour, but he's vanished.'

'I see. I am afraid that rather confirms my fears. It is also out of character. Please keep looking and try and catch the animal. I shudder to think what he would do if he meets poor Mr Symonds.'

Relieved his mistress was not angry, Jack risked a grin. 'I expect he is over on the downs somewhere, rabbit hunting. I'll go there again and take another look.'

After Jack's departure Sarah found a book to read and settled down, but she couldn't concentrate. Too much had happened. For the second time that day she wished Oliver was with her and she had been delighted and relieved to discover that Peters had ridden off to town to fetch him back. When he was there even the worst situations were more bearable.

The following morning Sarah was fully restored. Apart from a little residual stiffness, she could almost imagine yesterday's near miss had not occurred. She decided that politeness demanded she descend to Lord Fitzwilliam's quarters where she could offer her thanks for his kindness in person. She could also reassure him that neither she, nor Edward, had suffered lasting damage from the unfortunate mishap.

Edward was reluctant to accompany her. He had heard that his beloved pet was still missing and wanted to be allowed to go with Jack to search for him.

'Rags has been out all night on his own. He will be really miserable. I promise I will stay with Jack at all times, Mama. Sally can take me down to the stables, then you can go and visit Lord Fitzwilliam in peace.'

'Oh, very well, young man. But I must have your word of honour that you will not go on the beach alone to look for your dog.'

'I have already promised Papa and I do not break my word. You can trust me.'

Sarah bent to kiss him, flinching as her dress rubbed her injured shoulders. 'Sally, make sure Jack is at the stables; do not send Edward on alone, take him there yourself.'

Sarah checked her appearance, smoothed her hair and, with Beth walking sedately behind, headed downstairs to await her summons to the earl's sanctum. Although Lord Fitzwilliam had not proved to be too high in the instep, she had decided it would be politic to have her maid with her. An elderly gentleman might not wish to converse with a young woman who was unattended.

Edward walked ahead of Sally but remained within arm's reach as he had promised. They were half-way down the long flagged path when a housemaid hurried up. 'Sally, Mrs Mason has asked you to attend her directly.'

Sally stopped, undecided. She had promised Mrs Mayhew not to allow Edward to walk alone but she could not ignore a summons from such an august body as the housekeeper.

'Can I help, Sally? You seem bothered by something?'

'Oh, Mr Symonds you gave me such a start, coming out from behind the hedge like that.'

'Good day, sir. I'm going to the stables to help look for my dog, but now Sally has to go and see Mrs Mason.'

Mr Symonds smiled. 'I have just seen Jack on the downs, Master Edward. Shall I take you to him?'

'Oh, yes please, sir. That would be splendid!' Sally was not so sure. There was something about the swarthy manservant that made her skin crawl.

'There, Sally, you can go to see Mrs Mason and I can go and find Jack. My mother will be quite happy for me to go with Mr Symonds. He is Lord Fitzwilliam's personal servant, is he not?'

'Yes, Master Edward.'

Symonds gave her no choice. Still smiling, he grasped Edward's willing hand and disappeared back through the gap in a hedge from which he had made such an unexpected appearance minutes before.

Sally shrugged. If Master Edward was content to go, she supposed there was no harm done. She retraced her steps to the house and went to find out why the housekeeper had sent for her so urgently. As the side door closed behind her, three mud-spattered riders galloped into the stable-yard. Captain Mayhew, Jenkins and Peters had returned.

Oliver vaulted from the saddle and flung the reins across to Jenkins, who was profoundly grateful to be back on terra firma. Riding had never been a favourite of his, and riding *ventre à terre* for six hours had been a living nightmare. Oliver attempted to brush the worst of the travel grime from his clothes and satisfied he was clean enough to pass muster, set off for the house.

He did not run, it was not his object to draw attention to himself, but his long strides got him to the door before Jenkins had covered half the distance. He didn't pause to knock but just walked in. He took the stairs two at a time. Meeting Peters and hearing about the accident had added urgency to his mad gallop. He would not be happy until he saw Sarah and Edward safe and well, with his own eyes.

He burst into their shared rooms, startling the two chambermaids. 'Where are Mrs Mayhew and Master Edward?' His barked question further flustered the girls.

'I don't know where Mrs Mayhew has gone but Master Edward went to the stables to see Jack, sir.'

Oliver scowled. The two girls retreated further from the travel-strained man who had invaded their workplace. 'How long ago did Master Edward leave?'

'A short while only, sir. We passed the nursemaid and Master Edward on our way up.' She smiled nervously. 'They were on the back stairs, sir.'

'Thank you, you have been most helpful.' Oliver flashed them a smile and they instantly forgave him for his abruptness.

Where was Sarah? Should he go and look for her or go back to the stables to find Edward first? He decided Edward must be his priority. As he turned to leave he heard the door in the dressing-room open and someone hurry in. Sally appeared, her face tear-stained.

'Oh, Captain, sir, thank God you are back!'

'What is it, Sally? Calm yourself and tell me, at once.'

'Madam told me to stay with Master Edward all the time; she was worried after the accident yesterday and the dog turning nasty.'

'Where is Master Edward, Sally?'

'That is what I was coming here to tell Mrs Mayhew. A girl told me to go at once to see Mrs Mason but when I got there I wasn't expected at all. But that Mr Symonds has taken Master Edward away with him.'

'God's teeth! The devil he did!' Oliver ran from the room and pounded back downstairs. This was the worst possible news. He met Jenkins and Peters waiting on the steps. 'Symonds has Edward. Let us pray that we will find them in time.'

The two men raced back to the stables hoping to pick up the trail there. Billy said he had seen the pair heading for the beach about half an hour before. Peters held out his master's sword-belt and Oliver buckled it on. He turned and, shouting for Billy and Ned to follow him, ran full stretch towards the sea.

Sarah had been enjoying her time with Lord Fitzwilliam. He was a lively conversationalist and entertained her with amusing anecdotes from his youth. She spent the requisite thirty minutes and then politely rose, indicating that he should remain seated. She could not bear to see him struggle with his sticks and his valet was, for some reason, nowhere to be seen.

'I will bid you good day, my lord. Thank you for your time. I have enjoyed my visit immensely.'

He chuckled, a picture of benign amiability. 'Come again my dear Mrs Mayhew. And next time make sure that scamp of a son accompanies you. Young Edward has been very remiss. He has not been to see me today. There are still many things he needs to be instructed in.'

Sarah curtsied. 'I will make certain he attends you tomorrow, Lord Fitzwilliam.'

As they were walking along one of the interminable corridors upstairs, she stopped and glanced from the window. Something had attracted her attention; she was not sure what it was. She asked Beth to push up the window so that she could have a better view. She leant out and her heart plummeted. What she had seen was Oliver running as though his life depended on it, his sword at his side, closely followed by Jenkins and Peters, rifles in hands, and two grooms carrying pitchforks.

The spectacle would have been ridiculous was it not for the

look of desperation on Oliver's face. What was going on? Where were they all running to? She looked across the beach, shading her eyes from the blinding sun. For a moment she could see nothing out of the ordinary. Then, in the distance, she saw the twisted arms of the wreck and running away from it was a tiny figure in black, who could only be one person: Symonds, Lord Fitzwilliam's manservant.

Chapter Twenty-One

'MR Symonds, I can't see Jack on the downs, shall we call out to him?'

'No, Master Edward. I expect he is too far away to hear.' The man started to lead Edward towards the beach. 'The tide is on the way out. Would you like to explore the old wreck with me?'

'Yes. please, I would. Mama only said I could not go out alone. She could not object to me going out with you, could she?' Edward smiled up artlessly. 'I have wanted to look at it ever since we arrived at Westover, last week.' He bounced along beside the valet, quite forgetting his original quest for Jack and his dog.

The empty sands stretched invitingly, the retreating sea invisible over the horizon. The black twisted remains of the sunken ship seemed a long way away. Edward tried to stop but Symonds's hold tightened and he found himself propelled across the beach.

'You're going too fast, sir. I can hardly keep up.'

Symonds slackened his pace. 'I apologize, Master Edward. I was forgetting you have shorter legs than me. I am as keen to see the wreck as you are; it is years since I came out to look at it myself. I remember the night it went down. Would you like me to tell you about it?' Edward forgot his qualms in his eagerness to hear the gruesome story.

It took fully fifteen minutes' brisk walking to reach their

objective and the shoreline had shrunk to a smudge, barely discernible in the heat haze.

'Up you come, Master Edward. Hold my hand, the weed makes it slippery to climb.' Mr Symonds gave the child no chance to pull back. He picked him up and pushed him bodily up the side, giving Edward no choice. He either scrambled up the remaining few feet or tumbled back down to the wet sand.

Once on board Edward peered nervously into the black hole, which was all that remained. Now that he was here, he was not so sure it had been such a good idea. 'It is very dark down there, Mr Symonds. I'm not sure I want to explore inside.' He could hear the seawater trapped below slopping back and forth and unpleasant scuttling noises. He definitely regretted his impulsive decision.

Mr Symonds laughed heartily, the noise sounding false even to a boy as young as he was. 'Come along, Master Edward, we might find some treasure down there.' All Edward could see were twisted rotting crossbeams and nasty, dark, rank-smelling water. His desire to investigate vanished and he attempted to step away but found his passage blocked. He stumbled and cried out as a large hand shoved him forward and he fell into the bowels of the wreck.

He screamed as he hit the freezing water, thinking he was going to disappear under its black surface. But the water was only a few inches deep. Bruised and terrified he staggered to his feet, his thin muslin shirt and breeches soaked. He looked up, still not quite believing what had happened, expecting to see Mr Symonds climbing down to assist him.

What he saw caused him to whimper in terror. The man he had thought of as a friend was staring down at him with an expression of such malevolence, Edward could not fail to recognize it.

'Well, well! Now we have you! The tide has turned and in a short while it will be all over for you, my boy. My master can die happy knowing that his lands and title will go to a true Englishman and not a little blackamoor.'

Edward heard his abductor climbing back onto the sand and realized it was pointless to call out. He was alone and no one knew where he was. He had been told not to go near the wreck and he had given his word. Was God punishing him for his disobedience? How long did he have before the sea poured in and filled his prison? He stared hopelessly up at the only way out but knew that the sun-filled hole was too far away for him to reach.

A small amount of sunlight filtered in through the gaps in the planks and gave him just enough illumination to look around for something to climb on, but all the walls were slippery with weed. He sat down in the water and his sobs echoed forlornly around the abandoned ship.

Oliver saw on the horizon a spidery figure scrambling from the wreck and increased his pace. He heard pounding paws behind him and Rags shot past, his teeth bared and his hackles up, a fearsome snarl clearly audible. The dog reached the sand before him and raced off, his intention clear: Symonds was his quarry.

'Christ save us, the tide has turned,' Oliver gasped. 'I will not get there in time.' He tore of his sword-belt, jacket and boots and began a last desperate race against the sea.

'What about Symonds?' Jenkins called after him.

'Kill him.' Oliver replied.

'My pleasure, sir.' Jenkins had his rifle loaded and ready in seconds. He raised the gun to his shoulder, aimed, and squeezed the trigger. The two grooms watched in awe as the distant figure fell forward onto the sand, the ball killing him instantly.

Rags, seeing the man drop, changed direction and began to follow Oliver out to the wreck. His paws were splashing rhythmically in the rising water as he raced. Oliver kept his eyes firmly on the wreck, praying he would reach it in time. The incoming tide was lapping at his ankles and running was becoming more difficult. He reckoned he had five minutes to reach it and find Edward before the full force of the waves engulfed them.

He was near enough to shout. 'Edward, I am coming, hang on lad. I will have you out in a moment.' Was he too late? Had Symonds killed the child before he ran away? The water was at his knees and climbing rapidly. With a last desperate surge he reached the slippery black sides of the ship and started to climb, calling out as he did so. 'Edward? Edward, son, answer me if you can.' No answer, only the ominous gurgling of the incoming water as it gushed through the gaps in the beams and began to fill up the boat.

Oliver flung himself over the edge and into the darkness. For a moment he could see nothing then his eyes adjusted and he saw Edward's terrified face staring at him, the sea already up to his shoulders. With one scoop he snatched him up and held him above the water.

'Edward, Papa is here now, it is going to be all right. Trust me.' He felt the boys arms link in a vice-like grip around his neck and thanked God he had not been too late.

The water was up to his chest. He had to get both of them out of the hold if they were to have any chance of survival. In his determination to reach Edward he had jumped down without checking he was going to be able to get out again. Was this to be a fatal error? His only chance was to swim up as the level rose and pray he could get them out of the hole before the currents created by the water sucked them both back down to their deaths. He shifted his grip on Edward and used his free arm to keep their heads above water.

The sea lifted him and he kicked frantically. He could feel the terrifying force of the water as it raged into the confined space and, for an instant, feared he would not be strong enough. Then, like a cork, they were shot out of the hole and into the open sea. Where ten minutes before there had been sand, now all that stretched in any direction was water.

The wreck had already vanished under the sea. He held Edward's face above the waves and looked around; he couldn't see the beach. He had no idea which way to swim and knew his ability to keep them afloat was rapidly waning.

Then he felt something nudge his side and saw the shaggy face of Rags appear beside them. The dog swam strongly ahead and Oliver followed. Animals had an instinct for survival and he had to trust that. He had nothing else.

Then he felt a surge of power from behind and suddenly he and Edward were being carried along by the racing water. All he had to do was keep their heads clear and allow the sea to do the rest. Once they had broken free from the dangerous eddies surrounding the wreck the power of the incoming tide was carrying them to shore.

Minutes later he felt his feet touch the sand and bracing himself he started to wade through the water. He raised his head and could see the dunes a few hundred yards ahead. He knew he would have to run to try and beat the sea. If it overtook them again he would not have the strength to keep afloat. With his precious burden clasped to his chest he raced for safety.

Faintly he thought he could hear voices calling, but all his remaining strength and concentration was focused on this final effort. He felt his bare feet hit the dry sand and knew he was winning. Then the sand became dry underfoot and he realized he was safe. They were both safe. He collapsed to his knees, his chest heaving as he dragged air into his oxygen-starved lungs.

'Edward, you are safe now,' he croaked and slid the boy down to stand on his own feet. The boy's body flopped from his grasp and lay, apparently lifeless, on the sand. Oliver reacted by instinct. He threw the limp form over a raised knee and began to pound on his back, his fists moving from buttocks to neck and up again. Water gushed from Edward's gaping mouth but still he didn't move. Once, Oliver had seen a ship's surgeon breathe life back into a sailor who had been plucked half-dead from the sea. Could he possibly do the same? Desperately he flipped Edward over and laid him on the sand. Then he bent forward and covered the boys mouth with his own, blowing air into it. Nothing happened. Oliver tried again and again and he thought he felt faint movement of the boy's chest, then nothing. He sat back, snatching Edward up to cradle him, unconcerned that Jenkins and the grooms could see the tears flowing freely down his cheeks. He had failed. This precious child had died.

'Sir, Captain, sir, I swear the lad's breathing. Try him over your knee again. Let the water come out.' Jenkins's words pierced through his misery and he did as suggested. He pummelled the boy for a second, futile time and miraculously the tiny shoulders convulsed and water spewed from Edward's mouth and he coughed and drew a ragged, gasping breath of life-giving air.

Gently, Oliver righted the child and stroked his pallid cheeks. 'Thank God, Edward, you have come back to us.' He tried to stand but his legs would not respond. He felt a steadying arm under his elbow and regained his feet with his stepson in his arms breathing, but still unconscious. 'Run back, Billy, and raise the alarm. Peters go with him. Arrange for someone to fetch the doctor and then ask Mrs Mason to go up and tell Mrs Mayhew what has happened.'

Oliver was grateful for the sun's healing warmth and slowly his leaden limbs began to respond to his bidding more willingly. He than recalled that Rags had been swimming with him. 'Jenkins, send someone to look for the dog. He was out there with us. If it was not for him, I doubt I would have had the sense to swim away from the wreck. Edward and I owe our lives to that dog.'

'I will organize a search party as soon as we get you both back, sir.'

Oliver, from being frozen to the marrow, now felt the sweat trickling down his forehead. He blinked and shook his head. He feared that if he removed an arm to wipe his face, he would drop the boy. His strength was almost gone.

He had ridden the fifty miles from London hard, run several miles and swum another: it was no wonder he felt as though he was beginning to flag. Willing hands finally removed the child from his arms and, his part played, he fell forward unconscious onto the flagstones. The boy was carried, still inert, upstairs to be placed in the marital bed.

Sarah and Beth expertly stripped him and chafed his limbs with red flannel. The bed, in spite of the heat outside, had been warmed by hastily heated bricks. Sarah held her son's limp hand and called his name.

'Edward, darling, wake up. You are safe now, your Papa saved you.' The small cold hand moved slightly and the pale eyelids flickered open.

'Where is Rags? I want to see him, please.'

'Of course, my love. As soon as he is dry and clean, I will have him brought straight up.' Sarah prayed the searchers would find the dog alive and her lie would remain undiscovered. For the moment Edward was satisfied with her explanation and sank back into a semi-conscious state.

Sally appeared at the bedside. 'Beth and I will sit with Master Edward, madam. If you wish to attend to the captain.'

Sarah jerked round. 'The captain? Is he injured?' Sally and Beth exchanged glances. Beth spoke, trying to break the bad news as gently as she could. 'He is in a bad way, madam. He collapsed outside and has not regained his senses yet.'

Sarah suppressed the whimper of agony that threatened to escape. She prayed as she ran across the room. 'Please God, not Oliver. He is a good man, and I love him!' Jenkins was blocking her view of the bed and its occupant. The servant stepped aside and Sarah could see the man, she had only just realized, who meant more than the world to her. He was lying with closed eyes, his face as white as his sheets.

'Darling Oliver, please do not die. I love you so. and I do not wish to live my life without you.' Sarah threw herself on the bed and placing a hand on either side of Oliver's face lowered her head and kissed his cold lips.

To her astonishment his mouth opened under hers and two remarkably strong arms enfolded her. She was unceremoniously rolled across the bed until she was trapped beneath her husband, who was very much alive. When he finally raised his head Sarah had no breath to speak. She gazed, spellbound, into blue-grey eyes that blazed with love and sighed with pleasure.

She smiled, her face transformed. 'Oliver, I have been such a fool. I did not fully understand, until I thought I had lost you just how much you mean to me.'

He dropped his head and kissed her again; a slow, gentle exploration, with no sign of his previous urgency. He pushed himself up onto one elbow and traced the shape of her lips with one finger. With a lazy, contented smile he finally broke the charged silence.

'I have loved you for weeks, my darling. I have been waiting for you to recognize that you had been similarly smitten.'

Reluctantly Sarah sat up. 'I must return to Edward, he is still not fully recovered. I do not think he will get better until Rags is back with him.'

Instantly Oliver's face sobered. 'God, how could I forget? I am coming too. I must wash off some of the salt and change my clothes and then I will join you.'

'Are you sure you are well enough to get up? Beth thought you were at death's door.'

His mouth curved into a lopsided grin. 'I am sorry to have scared you. I merely swooned. It would appear to be a family failing!'

213

Sarah, who had regained her feet, shook out her crumpled skirts. Then a faint sound behind her made her jump and a fiery blush surged from her toes to her crown. She had forgotten that they were not alone. With horrified eyes she looked at Oliver, who openly laughed at her discomfiture. Jenkins grinned too, glad the captain and his missis had finally come to their senses.

'You are impossible, Oliver. I cannot imagine why I love you.'

Oliver swung his legs on the bed and prepared to stand up. 'Can you not, my darling? If you remain for a while longer I would be delighted to show you.'

Sarah stormed out of the room, bristling with righteous indignation. Oliver nodded, pleased that annoyance had replaced the pinched look on his wife's face. 'What did you do with the body, Jenkins?'

'It's stored in the barn, sir. What are you going to do about his lordship? He cannot be allowed to get away with it. He is behind all this.'

'I will deal with him later. The man is a cripple, without Symonds to do his dirty work he is helpless. But have two men guard his quarters, just in case.'

Sarah and Oliver sat quietly beside their sleeping son. The doctor had examined him and declared him in no imminent danger of death. However he warned that lung congestion and fever could set in, so they would have to wait and see. Occasionally the child opened his eyes and smiled at his anxious parents, asked yet again when his dog was coming. Then receiving no news of Rags fell back into a restless doze.

It was late in the afternoon when they heard voices and heavy footsteps approaching the door. Oliver frowned and stood up, alert to possible danger. It banged open and Jack, a grin splitting his face, walked in, an enormous, wet, hairy bundle in his arms.

'We found him, sir. He must have been washed ashore a mile or so up the coast. I've given him a bit of a clean-up but I thought as young Master Edward would want to see him right away, wet or not.'

Oliver pointed to the bed. 'Put him down on there, Jack, next to Edward.'

Sarah had been about to protest but the words died on her lips as her son reached out and buried his hand in Rags's sandy coat. The dog's long pink tongue flopped out and kissed the boy's face, then both fell into a deep, restorative slumber.

'I think we can safely leave them now, Oliver. Sally and Beth can watch Edward between them.' Sarah yawned and stretched, sitting still for so long had made her tired. 'I am going to take a stroll on the terrace, the fresh air will wake me up. Will you join me?'

Oliver didn't answer until they were in the corridor outside. 'There are still unresolved issues I must deal with, sweetheart. And forgive me, but I must insist you remain in your sitting-room for the present.'

Sarah nodded. 'I realize that you have to catch Symonds. I also understand that it was Lord Fitzwilliam who was behind all this, but I do not know why he should wish either of us harm.'

'Neither do I, but I am going to find out. And do not worry about Symonds, he is dead. Jenkins shot him.'

'Good! I would have done so myself if I had had the opportunity.'

Oliver was startled by his wife's unexpected comment. 'I seem to remember that you hate violence of any sort, Sarah. What has changed your opinion so radically?'

Sarah stood on tiptoe and kissed him. 'It is being married to you, my love. Some of your ruffianly tendencies must have rubbed off.' He pulled her into a fierce hug, returning her kiss in full, then released her and guided her, unresisting into the

215

sitting-room. 'Take care, Oliver. Lord Fitzwilliam might be a cripple but he can still hold a pistol.'

'I will be careful, sweetheart. I always am. Stay in here, whatever you hear, do you promise me?' Sarah did and Oliver bounded downstairs to confront the earl and discover the answers to the puzzle.

Chapter Twenty-two

THE sea continued to sparkle in the distance but Sarah's delight in the spectacle had gone. She wanted to return to Rowley Court and the green tranquillity of the countryside. To live in a house where the kitchens were not so distant that all the food arrived stone cold and where it didn't take an hour to walk from one's bedchamber to the gardens. She hated the fact that she was residing under the roof of the man who had been the instigator of all the murder attempts.

Although she and Edward were out of danger she still felt insecure and uncomfortable. She believed that she could never be happy living at Westover: it was too huge, too impersonal. There were so many staff it would be impossible to ever know them all by name.

Her eyes filled with unexpected tears. Would Edward's status mean they would be obliged to live here? She remembered what Oliver had said about responsibilities. Westover could not be left empty or the staff would be unemployed. Angrily she rubbed her eyes and straightened her shoulders and felt a sharp reminder of the previous day's misadventure.

What was Oliver doing downstairs? Would he kill the earl? Surely not in cold blood? He was not a murderer and, however evil, the man was old and a cripple. Oliver could have Lord Fitzwilliam confined in his quarters, guarded by his own men, otherwise what was to stop his lordship recruiting a second person to carry out his murderous instructions?

The soft swish of material on the polished floorboards made her pause in her restless pacing.

'Master Edward's awake, madam, and would like to see you.' Beth told her quietly.

'I expect he will be hungry. Please go down to the kitchen and find him some broth.'

'Would you like anything, madam? You have not eaten all day.'

Sarah considered. 'Yes, I would like some bread and cheese, and cold cuts. And we still have the fruit basket up here to accompany that.'

Edward, the dog still stretched out beside him, grinned happily as his mother entered. 'Rags likes being up here with me, Mama. Can he sleep here always? There is plenty of room for you as well.'

'I am not sharing my bed with a dog, my love, even if you wish to do so. And Rags may remain here for tonight only. Then he must return to the stable where he belongs.'

'You will have to sleep in Papa's room and then you will be kept awake by his snoring.'

Sarah felt her face colour; she hoped it would not be Oliver's snoring that kept her awake that night. 'Sally can sleep in here with you. We can have a truckle bed put up for her.'

Sally shook her head. 'No. there is no need, madam. The bed is big enough for six to sleep in comfort. I will put a bolster down the middle and still have plenty of room.'

'Thank you Sally. It will be easier for me to rest knowing that you are in here with Edward.'

'Where is Papa? I have something important to ask him.' Edward chimed in.

'He is busy downstairs, Edward. I am sure he will be back later to see you. Could you not tell me instead?'

'Oh, very well. But Papa will have the answer, he always does.'

'I am sure you are correct, my dear. What is it you wish to ask me?'

'After Mr Symonds pushed me into the hole he said something I did not understand. He said that the earl could now die happy knowing a blackamoor would not inherit the title. What do you think he meant, Mama?'

'A blackamoor?' She repeated, for a moment as puzzled as her son. Then it all fell into place, the reason behind the attacks suddenly became obvious. 'Do you remember me telling you about your great-grandmother?

Edward screwed up his face. 'That she was an Indian princess, and that is why I have darker hair and skin than you do?'

'Yes, darling, that is exactly what I mean. For us, such an important ancestor is a wonderful thing, but to Lord Fitzwilliam it was an insult to his title. He wanted Mr Fitzwilliam to inherit because his ancestors were all English. Even though you have only a small amount of Indian blood, to some people this would make you an unsuitable heir to a great estate.'

Edward mulled this extraordinary information over for a moment. 'I think Mr Symonds and Lord Fitzwilliam must be touched in the attic to think such a stupid thing.'

'I agree, Edward, you are absolutely correct.' She smoothly changed the subject not wishing her son to dwell on such an unpleasant notion. 'Are you hungry? I have sent for some broth for you.'

'I hope you have asked for something for Rags. He is hungry too, aren't you boy?' The dog thumped his tail, but was still too exhausted to raise his head from the pillow.

Oliver found Jenkins and Peters on guard outside the earl's private quarters. 'Any trouble, Jenkins?'

'None, sir. Not a peep from in there.'

'Can servants access the apartments from another entrance?'

'No, Captain, I sent Murray and Ned to guard the servants' door. No one has been in or out.'

'Come with me, both of you. We might not expect trouble, but it is as well to be prepared.' Oliver handed his pistol over to Jenkins and heard it being primed and cocked, ready for action.

The external door opened silently on well greased hinges and Oliver stepped in, ready, his eyes scanning every corner for a possible attack. The vast reception room was empty; Lord Fitzwilliam's high chair deserted.

Oliver gestured towards the closed doors at the far end of the room and silently the three men moved forwards with the ease of long practice. At the doors they stopped and Oliver pressed his ear against the wooden panel. Still no sound. He had never entered their quarry's private quarters and had no idea what labyrinth of rooms and passages might lie behind the door.

He clasped the polished knob and, standing sideways, using the door's bulk as protection. slowly pushed it open. The room was also empty. Three further closed doors faced them. This was obviously a vestibule. The thick carpet muffled their booted footsteps and Oliver whispered to his men.

'Murray, check the door on the left. Jenkins, you take the one on the right and I will go to the centre.' In unison they crept forward and repeated their previous cautious procedure.

Oliver carefully opened the central door and peered through the gap and then relaxed. 'In here, lads. No need to look any further.' He stepped into the room, a study, and walked across to examine the figure slumped across the desk.

'Saves us a job, Captain.' Jenkins observed dispassionately.

Oliver stared down at the man, his corpse already stiffening, and was unmoved. He noticed a paper open on the desk and picked it up. As he scanned the contents he understood why the Earl had been driven to end his own life. The letter was from an informant in London telling him that his plot had been discovered. Fitzwilliam had taken the only way out.

'At least the bastard did the right thing, in the end, sir.' Murray said quietly, unnerved by his captain's silence.

Finally Oliver spoke, his tone urgent. 'Get this cleaned up, Jenkins. Put the body in bed and cover up the head. No one else must come in here, is that clear?'

Puzzled, Jenkins nodded. Oliver looked at the blood-spattered walls and stained carpet. It was going to take more than a scrubbing to remove the evidence. 'Get rid of the carpet and replace it. Paint the walls, if you have to. I want this room to look unsullied. I will not have my son's inheritance tainted by this scandal.'

Jenkins began to follow the captain's reasoning. 'But what about the death certificate, sir? The doctor can hardly write natural causes, when half the man's head is missing.'

Oliver's smile did not reach his eyes. 'The quack will write what I damn well tell him to. I will announce that he died peacefully in his sleep tomorrow morning, after we have him safely banged up in his coffin.'

'I will get Billy and Jack to find the box. Nobs always have these things ready, so it shouldn't be hard to track it down.'

Oliver nodded towards the bloody remains. 'Clean the pistol he used and replace it in its case. Check all the doors are locked before you start. How long do you think it will take you?'

'If we work all night it will be done by morning, sir. I will send word up when we've finished.'

'Excellent. It is six o'clock now. It will not be dark for another four hours. Be careful how you go; this matter must be kept secret.'

He left his men to their grisly task and made his way back upstairs. He could hear the sound of laughing and the clatter of cutlery coming from Sarah's room. He quickened his steps

221

and walked in. For a moment he was too moved to speak. The sight of Sarah and Edward, sharing a plate of steaming broth, their dark heads touching, lifted his heart and temporarily banished his grim thoughts.

'I hope there's enough for me; I am famished.' Two heads jerked round at the sound of his laughing comment and two faces lit up with joy on seeing him. Sarah held out her hand, her face radiant.

'Come and join us, my love. The broth is, for once, hot and the bread freshly baked. Beth has fetched enough to feed all of us. There is plenty for you.'

The maid handed Oliver a full bowl and spoon and he perched on the edge of the bed to eat it. The meal was declared the most appetizing one that they had eaten since arriving at Westover. Edward yawned and rubbed his eyes.

'It is time we all got some rest, Edward. It has been a long and difficult day.'

'It is still light, Mama. Do you go to bed in the daytime too?'

'When we are tired, yes, my love, we do.' Oliver hugged his adopted son, knowing this would be the last night the boy would be known as Master Edward. In the morning he would be a different person; he would be Lord Edward Fitzwilliam, Earl of Westover.

Sarah kissed her son too. 'Sleep well, darling. Sally will be here if you need anything. And Papa and I will be next door. Goodnight and God bless.'

Oliver slipped his hand around her waist, drawing her closer. 'Goodnight, son.' holding his beloved wife to his side he led her through the communicating door and into the majestic bedchamber. With his free hand he turned the key behind him. 'Sarah, darling, look at me.' He placed his finger under her chin and gently forced her to meet his eyes. 'If this is moving too fast for you I will understand. I can sleep elsewhere, if that is what you wish.'

She smiled, her eyes huge. 'No, it is not that. I love you Oliver, and do want to be your true wife. But I find I cannot relax until I know exactly what happened downstairs.'

'The earl is dead. He blew his brains out.'

'Is that a good thing?'

His mouth twisted wryly. 'I honestly do not know. If word ever comes out that he committed suicide Edward's name will be besmirched. It can take generations to live down such a scandal.'

'Do you believe he did it to cause us more grief?'

'I am certain of it, sweetheart. But with luck we will come out of this unscathed.' He explained exactly what he had set in motion downstairs and Sarah was impressed.

'Lord Fitzwilliam was in his eighties. I am sure no one will question his sudden death. I suppose we will have to stay here now, at least until you have sorted everything out here?'

'I am afraid so, my love. But things will be different now that I am in charge. I promise we will return home as soon as we can.'

'Do you truly think of Rowley Court as your home, Oliver?'

'I felt I belonged there the moment I saw you, my darling.'

Sarah rested her head on his chest. 'I am so lucky you found me, Oliver. I believe that tonight in spite of everything that has happened, I am the happiest woman in the world.'

Oliver's arms tightened and he murmured softly into her hair. 'I promise you, my darling, that in a very short while, I am going to make you even happier.'